THE DEATHBED CONFESSIONS

Published September 2024
By Indies United Publishing House, LLC

ISBN: 978-1-64456-756-2 [Hardcover]
ISBN: 978-1-64456-757-9 [Paperback]
ISBN: 978-1-64456-758-6 [Kindle]
ISBN: 978-1-64456-759-3 [ePub]
ISBN: 978-1-64456-760-9 [Audiobook]

Library of Congress Control Number: 2024917237

INDIES UNITED PUBLISHING HOUSE, LLC
P.O. BOX 3071
QUINCY, IL 62305-3071
www.indiesunited.net

This book is dedicated to two Kate's.
Without them, writing would be impossible for me.
In fact, without them I might have trouble being a
fully functioning adult

I also want to thank,
Susan, John and Kenny for their help as well.
And most especially, thank you Lisa
Thank you

THE DEATHBED CONFESSIONS

Thomas Quinn Mysteries
Book One

MICHAEL DEEZE

INDIES UNITED PUBLISHING HOUSE, LLC

890547

When the prison gate slammed shut behind him, Tom Quinn flinched. He flinched again when the one in front of him slid open to a slow-motion 'clang' at the end of its travel.

"This way." The guard placed a hand on his shoulder and directed him forward into a long, brightly lit concrete hallway where another gate awaited at the far end. Only a few steps into the hallway, the last gate clanged shut and he could feel flop sweat soaking into his shirt. This time there was activity on the other side of the upcoming gate. People dressed in the hospital scrubs of medical staff moved around behind long glass windows beyond the gate.

"Open on 19!" shouted the guard behind him. The

gate clanked and then slid slowly open.

"Left."

Tom Quinn turned left.

"I'll take that jacket and lay your case on the table in front of you please, your watch, rings and any jewelry I can't see."

Tom Quinn shrugged out of his jacket, then after hesitating, he loosened his tie and dropped that on the table as well, next to his briefcase.

"FBI Agent Thomas Quinn, here to see prisoner 890547."

"Oh…he's been pretty specific. He wants no visitors."

"I bet! Half of Chicago wants him dead, and I don't blame 'em either." Then he softened, "Listen, the Feds want to get a few statements from him, you know, maybe wind up a case or two that's still out there so they sent this 'pencil neck.'"

"I'm standing right here." Thomas was insulted.

The orderly looked him up and down and smirked, unimpressed.

"That'll be fun. Hope you've got fire insurance um," he consulted the sign-in log, "…Agent Thomas Quinn. He's gonna burn you down."

"I'm pretty sure that I'm no threat. I'd just like to ask him a few questions." Tom Quinn pulled himself up to his full five-foot-nine-inch height and tried to meet the guard's steady gaze.

"Okay kid, but get your seat belt fastened. You're about to meet Harry Beech, and may god have mercy on your soul."

Thomas Quinn

My sister Lily died on my fourteenth birthday. At the time, I forgot all about it and missed the date completely, only to realize it weeks later. Lily had been my partner and my friend. Irish twins we were, her only nine months older than I but miles smarter and pretty where I was homely. It had been a fluke, something for my parents to watch but nothing any of us believed could be actually fatal. She had a hole in her heart, something that was supposed to close as she grew, but then it hadn't. Instead, she had become weaker and weaker. At the end, she could only lie on the couch while I did my best to entertain her. Then she had simply closed her eyes and gone to sleep and I lost my friend. My mother and father shooed me from the room while my mother cried and my father made phone calls. I locked myself in the bathroom and set the toilet paper on fire.

Lily had been the last sibling. Joshua had gone first. Blood poisoning after stepping on a rusty nail. He was stiff as a board when he stopped breathing. Gwen died of the whooping cough and so did Donny. But Lily was the last straw; Ma was never the same after that. She lost direction and disappeared into herself. Eventually, she found her excuse and when the cancer came, she embraced it. Within months she too was gone and she left me.

|||||||||||||||||||||||||||||||||||||||||||

I had chosen not to walk the stage or shake hands with the academic bureaucrats. I was getting my Master's degree and no handshake or piece of paper, no matter how well framed it was going to be, could tell the tale of what a struggle it had been. I spared myself the smarmy graduation ceremony with the proud parents and grandparents taking group photos all over the campus. I didn't have anyone who would have attended the ceremony anyway. No proud parents, no fawning girlfriend. I gave the registrar my forwarding address and went home early to contemplate my bleak future.

I had graduated from high school only a month after my father had died. I had no expectations of college; tuition, room and board put it out of reach. At the last career day before graduation, I stopped at the Army recruiter's table. The fantasy of going to college on the government's dime sounded pretty good to me. I didn't investigate further; I signed up for ROTC. Four and a half years later I had looked into the blinding blowing sands of the Iraqi desert and watched the men of my squad die. I had been one of the last ones to fall, but I had fallen none the less.

I did their rehab; I ran on their treadmill. I took their pills. I took my sessions with their psychiatrist. I passed and they put me back on the street. Back on the street with no place to go and nothing to do.

My counselor assured me that a Master's degree would guarantee a good job in law enforcement, especially law enforcement that didn't necessarily involve guns and explosives. I was accepted to a relatively prestigious school thanks largely in part to a honorable discharge and a bunch of ridiculous medals for things that I may or may not have done alone. With the help of two almost full-time jobs, I was able to finally earn a degree in Forensic Psychology. A great degree in a narrow field but with a career arrow pointed nowhere in particular.

I had mailed countless resumes and received several tepid responses but nothing with any meat on its bones. I went back to my small upstairs studio apartment and my bartender's job at night and waited for the mailman every day like my life depended on it, which in a sordid sort of way—it did.

And that's when the Federal Bureau of Investigation came calling.

Harry Beech

The world had caught up to Harry Beech on a beautiful spring morning. Those magical mornings in late spring when the air is cool and the dew is heavy and you can just catch a faint glimpse of your breath. Harry had missed the nuance; he'd been preoccupied. On that magnificent June morning, police responded to a 911 call in a quiet residential neighborhood on the west side of town. When they arrived they found Harry sitting in a swing rocker on the front porch of a neat two-story frame home at the end of a cul-de-sac. Harry still had the phone in his hand.

The front door was wide open, braced by the body of a man lying flat on his back, his feet extended out onto the porch. He lay in a pool of his own blood. His dead eyes were last focused on the small hole that had sprouted in his forehead. At the end of the entry hallway, another inert form lay across the back of a recliner: a woman, her sightless eyes gazing down at the still form of a child in her arms. The child, also deceased, apparently killed by the same bullets that had killed the woman. Then, as if the tragedy wasn't enough already, in the kitchen, a small toddler lay inert on the counter, its head face down in the full kitchen sink. The faucet still ran, and the water spilled across the flooded kitchen floor. Next to the child on the counter was a Ruger .38 caliber revolver; all cylinders appeared to have been fired.

Harry Beech had been convicted on four counts of homicide, although no motive could be established. The defense rested after only one day of testimony, and Harry Beech refused to testify in his own defense or to utter one word about the incident.

Due to the heinous nature of the crime, additional penalties were exacted by the judge beyond the jury's recommendations and he received four life sentences to run consecutively. Harry had requested the death penalty, but they deemed that he didn't deserve that kind of mercy and instead gave him no hope for parole.

Introductions

Now Harry was finishing his life sentences, all four of them at once. His cancer was advanced and the handwriting was on the wall. He would be getting out but leaving feet first. They say when someone dies, it's like having a library burn down. My station chief was afraid that Harry's library would burn down before Harry felt like telling anyone all the stories hiding somewhere inside him. Most specifically, the many cases, still technically open cases, that had never been solved and had at least a tangential relationship with Mr. Beech. The chief reasoned that Harry had nothing to lose now and that maybe he could unburden his conscience and help us out in the long run. And maybe give some families peace of mind after so many years of doubt. And maybe he'd be willing to share some of these secrets with the new guy.

A lot of maybes.

Harry you see, had been around a long time before the incident that got him convicted. Harry had been a well-known antagonist on the streets of Chicago for many years. He, at times, would seem to be involved in some crime, major or minor, but then, he would recede from view, and there was always insufficient evidence to take Harry's involvement anywhere beyond suspicion. The suspicions were multiple and frequent, yet Harry had never come to justice or even seen the inside of a courtroom beyond arraignment and bail posting. He seemingly had a guardian angel, and he had always walked away. Until the fateful spring morning when his involvement was blatantly obvious, and his guardian angel turned her back on him.

I stood in the narrow hallway, looking at him through the glass of his isolation suite. He was propped up in a half-seated position. From his file, I knew how old he actually was, but he appeared much older than his years. His face was all sharp angles; a hard jawline, high sharp cheekbones, and a broad ridge above his eyes made his eyebrows seem overly prominent. His lips were in a tight line, and his face seemed tight behind a nasal cannula inserted in large nostrils. Below his legs had emerged from beneath the bedsheets and appeared shrunken and overly skinny. Large, purplish bruises appeared randomly over much of the surface of his legs and forearms.

"The bruises are from the blood thinners he's on. It's not because of anything we did in here." Was the orderly's response to my questioning look. "He's on a shitload of pain medicine, probably in a lot of pain all the time still, but he don't talk about it. Shit, he probably hasn't said ten words since he got down here. Just lays there staring out through the glass. Kinda' creepy, if you know what I mean."

I'd looked at Harry's mug shots; they had spanned a few decades. A time lapse of the aging process in one man. Always well dressed, but you didn't notice that at first; what you noticed was the relentless and riveting gaze of his hawklike eyes from beneath hard brows. It was not the face that you wanted to meet on a dark street corner. The face I looked at through the glass window hadn't changed since his last photograph. It was daunting, even with his eyes closed, and it made me hope I wasn't in over my head. I pushed open the door and entered, but not before noting that his left wrist was handcuffed to the bedframe.

Once in the room, I found myself trying not to make a sound. As quietly as I could I set my briefcase down and sat in the plastic chair in the corner, content for the moment to let him sleep and not risk jarring him into wakefulness. The room was packed with the gantries and machines that accompany the very sick. A white robot machine in the corner clicked and wheezed, breathing in and out with measured rhythm. A display of instruments beeped and ticked as cursers ran across screens with numbers above his bed. All of the wheezing, ticking and beeping somehow seemed hypnotic as I waited.

"What?" His voice wasn't the least bit sleepy.

"What?"

"What do you want?"

"I'm Agent Thomas Quinn of the FBI. I'd like to ask you a few questions, Mr. Beech."

"Get lost."

He had never opened his eyes, but it seemed he hadn't been asleep after all.

"I'd like to. To be honest, I'd really like to, but they will probably just send me back again."

"See ya' next time then punk. Roberto will let you back out."

And with that, the interview was over.

Frozen Minutes

The orderly/floor nurse finger tapped the IV drip and then wrote something on his clipboard. He then scanned the numbers on the blip machine and wrote something else down.

"What time is it Roberto?"

He gave me a terrified look, then looked down at Beech.

"There's no time in here. Harry made me tape up the wall clock. Then we had to take it down altogether. He doesn't want to know what time it is. I'm not supposed to talk about time in here."

"Oh?" I chuckled a little, "I supposed he'll just jump up and kick your ass maybe?"

It was the third time I was sitting in the uncomfortable

chair in the corner. Harry had continued to play possum as usual, so when Roberto came in to chart the patient's vital signs, I was glad for a little change.

"Listen, I'm not gettin' crossways with Harry Beech. He said no clocks, so there's no clocks. You want to know what time it is you go out in the hall." He fiddled with the tubes and cords and then turned back to me. "How do you know my name anyway? I never told you."

"Harry told me." I nodded at his look of disbelief.

"That's because he stole my ID and nametag last month. That's how he knows it. Dammit, I knew it was him! Goddammit Mr. Beech."

"What?" I asked

"Yeah, like I know he did it. Who else? I turned this room upside down and inside out but I couldn't find it. It was an absolute shitstorm trying to explain how I lost it. This guy here, don't turn your back on him. Ever! Ain't that right Harry?"

"That is correct Roberto." Harry opened his eyes and looked at me, "You should have warned him before this."

"He actually pulled out his IV once" Roberto continued, "and he was using it as a lockpick for the handcuff. If the alarms hadn't all triggered, he'd have bled out in just a few minutes."

I had been sitting in the damn plastic chair, sweating my ass off, freezing from the waist up and staring at this breathing corpse for over a week, and now suddenly he's having a conversation like a normal human being. His voice was deep and mellow but came out in a whisper, and he formed the consonants carefully so that the full value of each word was realized.

"Yes, that would have been a terrible shame. Bleed

out in a hospital room and maybe cheat the hangman today just so I could shake hands with him tomorrow instead."

"And that's why our friend here, Mr. Beech, is handcuffed; he's a slippery eel even with one hand tied behind his back. He stole Phillip's, the night nurse, the same week. Actually, that's the only thing that saved my ass. That is that Phillip lost his only days after I'd lost mine. We never found 'em, but we know he's got 'em, or at least had them."

"I am saddened by your recriminations Roberto. With little or no evidence, yet you persist in this charade to cover your own lack of proper stewardship."

"Why d'ya talk that way to me Mr. Beech. I don't understand half of what you say sometimes."

"He said you're making up the story." I was still thunderstruck by the conversation. "I'm inclined to agree, doesn't sound plausible."

"Oh yeah, ask him why he had to be handcuffed huh? Ask him. . .no? He's handcuffed to the bed because he climbed up on that cabinet over there and pulled the clock down off the wall. That's why there isn't a clock in here. He was so agitated he had to be sedated, but he got his way, no clocks. But we also learned our lesson, and we and Mr. Beech have an understanding and a fancy bracelet to make sure he keeps his share of the bargain."

"You're just raising the bar for a little fun, that's all Roberto. The game is afoot. But that's enough for now. If you're finished with your rounding, you should move along."

"Oh thank you sir, so happy to be dismissed by your highness." He raised his eyebrows at me, shrugged, then turned and left the room, locking the door behind him.

"Why? Why bother stealing the ID's? You can't use them."

"Oh, I was hoping you'd left with him."

He plucked the sheet, shifted his feet and rocked his head from side to side. I thought he was done talking, but then, after a long pause, he spoke again.

"I've studied the Tao and I spend one-half of each day in meditation, contemplating the aberrant life form growing inside of me that is taking my life a millimeter at a time from me. That is tiring. Occasionally my mind wishes for recreation, perhaps a puzzle to solve, or just some pranking. It's entertaining, although I do acknowledge that it's also rather shallow."

"But why?"

He turned his head on the pillow and looked out from under the deep brows, "Because otherwise dying would just be boring.

Little Black Book - Harry

After the kid left, I spent some time thinking about him. He was earnest, but his enthusiasm was tempered. He had obviously seen some of what life has to offer, and it had left a mark. It was laughable, a little, that he had taken such an interest in the whole nametag/ID card thing. He didn't have anything better to do while he sat there in his chair, that was true, but he'd been genuinely offended that I had anything to do with it.

He probably had some idea of what a real 'bad guy' was like. His image most likely didn't leave room for grade school hijinks or petty thievery. Too bad, there's room for both in the same life. I remember when I was his age, the world seemed a lot more serious than it does these days. These days when it's much more a life and death situation. Those days it was easier to see the right and wrong. At least I thought so—back then.

The place stank of stale beer, cigarettes—and the air tasted like regret. The dim lighting masked the dated saloon fixtures and clientele from deeper scrutiny equally. Without exception, the figures leaning over their drinks were solitary, alone with their thoughts, or guilt—or both.

People didn't come to a place like this for pleasant conversation or the ambiance. There was no jukebox to liven the evening. The only sound, the muffled thump of filled glasses on the scarred wooden bar top or the rattle of whiskey bottles being returned to the shelf, broke the quiet. A silent hockey game played on the television mounted above the cash register at the end of the bar. The bartender knew how to mind his own business, and so did everyone else. This place was the place you go at the end of a chapter in the book of your life or at the beginning of the next one. It was a place to contemplate what went wrong.

Looking down the long bar from my stool at the far end, I knew every single one of them. I didn't know them personally or the names they went by, but I knew them; I knew who they were. These were my kind of people or had been. These were the reprobates of society, petty criminals, wife beaters, and the socially reprehensible characters who populated the back streets of our city. They were not homeless bums or vagrants; they had money in their pockets. How the money got in their pocket was nobody's business but their own. These were the people who made one fear the darkness or regret it.

I had been one of them for a time. Like them, I had thought there was nothing wrong with the lifestyle, that good or evil depended on which end of the shit stick you had grabbed hold of. I had believed that in life, you got what you got, and if this is what you got, then so be it. But the lifestyle was unforgiving, and sooner or later they would all succumb. Sooner or later, the devil got his due and they all knew it. I had walked into the darkness, and had met it face to face. The darkness knew my name too.

There had come a time when the light went on in my head. I had seen the handwriting on the wall and had hopefully begun to change my future. I no longer walked the back streets in the dark of night and the money in my pocket now came from a legitimate paycheck because she had helped me see a better way. But she, like most things in my life, was no more.

Places like this were still a comfort to me. This stool at the end of this bar with the wall behind me had been my seat, earned by contest and jealously guarded. No one fucked with me on this stool because I had fucked with each and every one of them at one time or another. They knew me well even though I was rarely seen here anymore. They knew my face, and they knew not to fuck with me. They knew that I wasn't here for the conversation either. The beer was cold; it was warmer here than out on the slushy winter street, and I had no place else to go tonight.

I had been here long enough to fill my bladder and after scraping my change off the bar, I pushed back and stepped to the toilet at the end of the hallway. This wasn't the kind of place that featured lemon-scented 'His' and 'Hers' restrooms. The 'restroom' was a toilet in a room with a small sink stand, a mop bucket and a musty wet mop as an air freshener. The toilet had plenty of grime and shit on it and in it, but when I flushed, it all went down and not up for a change.

Turning toward the sink stand, my boot caught against something down at the base of the toilet and it slid out into the dim light of the bare overhead bulb. A small black book. A small black book that someone had lost or left behind, probably while he dropped a deuce and his pants were down. I picked it up.

It looked like the kind of little book that bookies carry to keep track of their bets. I pocketed it and headed back out into the bar. With a look to the bartender, I made my way through and toward the front door and stepped out onto the sidewalk. Down the block, I unlocked my car and climbed in. Inside, with the overhead light on, I opened the little book, thinking there was bound to be a 'Finder's fee' for returning a bookies' client list. Inside there were no long lists of numbers or names. No race numbers at Washington Park. Inside was something entirely different.

With growing amazement, I flipped back and forth from page to page. Inside, in neat, careful Catholic-school penmanship, were pages of descriptive prose. A date, a name and a chapter devoted to the rape and torture of a woman or girl in graphic detail. As I read, I had first suspected it to be fantasy fiction, but with each entry it became increasingly obvious that it was fact, not fiction. It was a documentary of sickness written by a serial psychopath.

With each entry, the acts seemed to become ever more heinous, and near the back of this little black notebook, the last subject had not survived. The last entry's date had been yesterday. Her name had been Grace, and Grace had been eleven years old.

Closing the book, I closed my eyes and leaned my head back against the headrest. I hated this. I hated this feeling; this knowledge that things like this continued to fall into my lap. I hated that I had no choice. I hated that action was necessary and that I was compelled to supply it. Most of all I hated that I was one of them, one of the scum, perhaps not as much anymore, but once I had been one of them—the takers of souls.

Now I had become a worse thing, if that was even possible. I did not indulge in the self-righteous thinking of right or wrong, but I knew a heinous act when I saw it. I knew there was no need to balance the scale, both in justice and atonement. I knew that I had a lot to apologize for but I didn't need any of that to justify what needed to be done today. Opening the car door, I put one boot on the ground, knowing what would come next, angry at the circumstance and the friend that I was about to make.

Once back in the bar, the bartender acknowledged my return with the slightest lift of his chin and set a fresh beer glass down at my place. I signaled him to approach with a crook of my finger and when he leaned an elbow on the bar across from me, I showed him the book.

"Found this on the floor back in the shitter. Best see if it belongs to anybody." Before he could take it from me, I pulled it back and made eye contact with him. "But if anybody wants it, don't let 'em have it; bring it back to me." I handed him a twenty.

He didn't reply, just took the book and walked along the bar. Showing it to each patron but without explanation. The third person looked surprised and slapped his back pocket, then looked thunderstruck. He reached for it immediately, but the bartender pulled it back and kept walking. Once he'd done the circuit, he brought the book back and set it in front of me. He raised one eyebrow and cocked his head back toward the surprised fellow whose eyes had never left him.

"Is there gonna be trouble?"

"Nope, just want to make sure it's goin' to the right guy."

"If there's trouble, you take your business outside. Got it?"

"No trouble Jake."

The fellow down the bar had started to develop a twitch and finally couldn't contain it anymore. With a violent push, he left his stool and hurried back to where I was just getting interested in my fresh beer.

"Hey you found my book! Can I have it?"

"There oughta be a finder's fee."

"A finder's fee? Uh, yeah, sure. Like what?"

"I'm gonna need another beer pretty quick; let's start with that."

"Great, sure. How 'bout my book?"

"Pull up a seat. Nobody sits back here usually, kind a lonesome."

"Uh okay," He looked around my little corner of heaven. "You sure?"

"Pull up a seat, and we'll talk about that book. What'dya say?"

"The book, what about the book?"

"I looked at some of the stuff in there."

He was a good-sized guy, big shoulders but with a couple of rolls around his middle and a few days growth of beard going, but I watched the color drain out of his face just the same.

"You read some of it?"

"Yeah, you know. I was sittin' on the pot back there, so I flipped through a few pages. I was impressed, gotta say, I'm a big fan," I did a half turn on the bar stool and faced him. "If half that stuff is true man, you're a fuckin' artist."

"Uh an artist? What do you mean?"

"Well, I didn't get to read a lot, but what I read… Wow…those bitches…you know...like they got what they deserved, it looked like. And you were so creative! I'm just saying, I'm impressed."

"Yeah? You mean that?"

"Yeah, I do. Say, how about that beer? Oh, and a shot too? That should be included. After all, you wouldn't want to lose a book like that, right?"

"Yeah sure." He signaled the bartender for another round for both of us. "You think I'm an artist?"

"I really do. So, tell me more, I gotta know, how'd you get 'em? What'dya do with 'em when you're finished? You know, I'm getting a little excited just thinkin' about it." I winked at him, "If you know what I mean."

"It's not easy, you know. You gotta plan, you gotta watch 'em."

The bartender brought our new drinks and he waited until he moved back down the bar before continuing. Scooting closer on the edge of his seat and warming up to his audience of one.

"Yeah, like you gotta learn their habits and stuff. You can't just let yourself get careless. It's hard; takes a lotta plannin' ya know. You gotta really get to know 'em. Doesn't just happen overnight."

"I bet, geez, the suspense must be murder."

"Murder? What do you mean by that?"

"No, it's just a figure of speech. I just mean it must be hard to wait until the time is just right. How do you do it? Wait I mean."

"Oh, it is hard," He took a drink from his new beer, and I threw back the shot. I signaled the bartender to keep them coming. "You gotta have a lot of self-control. You gotta be in charge. Be the boss. The more you watch 'em, the more you learn what bitches they are. You learn to hate them more every day."

He was still talking when the bartender gave last call.

By now he was in no shape to drive anymore and I was his new best friend. Back out on the street, I offered him a ride home. I hinted, and he insisted that we make a slight detour so he could show me where he had left little Grace. It was a pleasant spot, under a viaduct that spanned a drainage ditch filled with trash and litter, close enough to the river so you could smell it at the back of your throat.

The police won't find him—or his little black book. I put him in the ground. The book was the last thing I threw into the hole with him before I filled the dirt back in. Afterward, I left little Grace where the authorities could find her in the morning.

He was surprised when I sent him to hell. I'll join him there one day. The darkness knows my name.

Greetings and Salutations

I sat in the uncomfortable plastic chair and tried to make my butt comfortable. I knew he wasn't sleeping. I'd figured that much out during my first and second visits. Eventually, he would tell me to get lost or just start snoring, but I waited anyway. The little white sentinel in the corner wheezed in and out, and the little blips coursed across their screens. Nothing changed in this room, day or night.

"Gotta name Agent Quinn?"

"What? Ye…yes. It's Thomas…Tom."

"Irish?"

"On my father's side, German and Polish on my

mother's."

"Get lost punk. No wait," he lifted his handcuffed arm palm out, "You close to them?"

"No."

"Why not?"

"My dad's gone, my mother too. She wouldn't have liked my job."

"She shouldn't." He pushed the button to raise his bed into a sitting position. "I had a family once. A great big family. People that I honestly loved and who loved me. But that's all gone now. The leopard couldn't change its spots, and I left it behind. But for a time, it was the only thing that mattered to me, and I fiercely defended it. But karma is a bitch as they say, and good deeds and bad deeds all have a price. Sometimes, that price is just money, and sometimes it's the most precious thing you can imagine. But the bill comes due, and there's nobody else standing at the cashier's window but you, you know kid."

The Leak

It had been a longer than usual drive. A November snow squall had blown in off Lake Michigan right during rush hour. The changeover from wet October to wet November in Chicago was always unpredictable and usually uncomfortable. The squall marked the change-over from autumn to winter and in Chicago that could mean anything. The proximity of the lake could bring rain in February and blizzards on Thanksgiving. Today it had reduced visibility to white-out conditions and packed itself into a glaze of slippery ice-covered roads at all the worst places, targeting the highest traffic areas. In no time, medians and ditches had become populated with hapless commuters, victims of fender-benders and their own sense of hurry.

I had white-knuckled all the way into the city and county lockup. My twice weekly trip all the way down to my usual ass-killing plastic chair in the antiseptic hospital room was in its third week. All that so I could sit and watch Harry Beech ignore me.

As usual, I had surrendered my hat, coat, and phone at the front desk check-in. Now back in my customary butt paralyzer of a chair, I had a chill from snow down the back of my neck and the chilly hospital room. I settled in and made my greetings to the little wheezing robot in the corner and waited. I questioned why I wasted my time and the Bureau's money making this useless trip, but so far, there hadn't seemed to be an off-ramp.

The orderly had informed me that there was no change in his condition, that he was non-communitive and that he seemed lethargic today. This was no surprise because he was always non-communitive and always sleeping, which is the very definition of lethargic. I knew what lethargic meant and was pretty sure that lethargic was how Harry Beech spent most of his time. I had yet to see him move more than the slightest shift of position. That was with the exception of his expressive eyebrows. Harry didn't waste any energy on movement of any kind. He could speak volumes with just his eyebrows, a study in psychological efficiency.

I had even given a thought today to bring a book to read, but then had forgotten it in my desk. I leaned back and stared at the ceiling, the beeping gantry behind his bed, and folded my arms, ready for long hours of meditation. That's when I found out today would be different.

"I heard they found old Billy Duggar."

"What?" I was totally unprepared for conversation; any conversation.

"Well?"

"Um yeah." It had not been our crime scene, local jurisdiction, but Billy had raised a few eyebrows and an FBI detail had been dispatched to assist. I had actually been one of the agents at the crime scene. Billy Duggar had been in his fifties, a member of the Knights of Columbus at Our Lady of Grace and a member of the American Legion post in the neighborhood. He'd been five days short of his thirty-second wedding anniversary. He had taken two small caliber shots to the back of his head and two more to the front. There was not a single file open on Billy Duggar; he had been a fine, upstanding member of the community. Law enforcement was scrambling for an explanation, but there didn't seem to be one.

That had not always been the case; Billy had a few files long ago. Billy had been somebody back in the old days, a made man as they say. But Billy had cleaned up his act once he got married. He'd gotten respectable thirty-odd years ago.

I looked at Harry. He raised one eyebrow in question, then I looked out through the glass of the isolation room as the orderly shuffled past. Isolation means isolation; where did he find out about Billy I wondered.

"So? How'd you know that?"

"Bad news travels fast."

"Did you know him? I was at the scene yesterday, no clues, nothing."

"Professional. Small caliber? .22 or .32 from a revolver. No brass to clean up. No shoeprints. Probably on cement or asphalt. Small caliber, no through-and-through, no ricochet."

"How…how do you know that?"

"Geez. Do you get paid to be stupid?"

Again, I looked out at the orderly as he passed the window again. Standing up I knocked on the glass and waived him into the room.

"Yes sir?"

"Harry is telling me about a murder that occurred recently out in Westmont. How's he getting his intel? Nobody is allowed in this wing unless it's official business. How does he know this stuff?"

"I don't know what you mean sir. Nobody is allowed to talk to anyone on the wing except one of us."

"Oh yeah? Where's your I.D. tag? If it's not in this room, where'd it go?"

"That's a mystery sir. I don't know."

He looked earnest but nervous. His feet were shuffling in place and he was picking at a scratch on the back of his hand. Quantico had taught me how to read people and Roberto was having issues. I considered just arresting him and sweating him down at the Bureau but I had a better idea.

"I don't give a shit if Harry has a visitor once in awhile, but I worry about his safety. If something were to happen to him, something that didn't quite smell right, that wouldn't look too good for you now would it? You'd be an accessory."

Sweat was starting to bead on his forehead, in spite of how chilly it was in the room. I glanced at Harry. His eyes were open for a change and he was boring a hole right through the poor guy. Roberto alternated between glancing at Harry Beech and not making eye contact with me.

"No sir…it's not like that."

"Then how is it?"

"Nobody comes to see Mr. Beech. Nobody."

"How's he get his news then?"

"I'll lose my job. Nobody comes to see Mr. Beech."

"It's okay, tell him Roberto. He's pretty harmless."

Roberto, the orderly, looked at Harry, then me and then he nodded.

"I'm gonna burn no matter what. Fuck you Mr. Beech, I'm gonna burn cuz' a you."

"Just tell him Roberto, I don't think he really cares that much."

I was surprised and my face showed it. Harry just shrugged—with his eyebrows.

"Just tell him."

Roberto turned away from me and looked out into the hallway through the glassed wall.

"We got these two guys. Um…you know. Uh…lifers. They're too old for GenPop ya' know. So they don't go to Marian; they're just here. Christ, they've been here since forever. They come down to mop up…couple times a day. At shift change…you know. Like when Phillip comes and takes over for me or vice versa. Time don't matter to these guys, so the time of day, early or late, they don't care. They do a good job, always whistl'n and hummin.' They take their time ya' know. Wipe down the counters, even dust the light fixtures. They're like first rate, always in a good mood."

He glanced over his shoulder and smiled out of the corner of his mouth. "Ya know?"

"Okay, I got it."

"Well they're not supposed to come in here. Mopping and cleaning up in here's supposed to be my job, uh our job, me and Phillip, but they do a really good job ya' know. They're…um…diligent, you know so a couple times they clean up Harry. Then a couple more times, then pretty soon twice a day. I'm sorry Agent Quinn, it just got away from us and then we couldn't report it without getting in some serious shit."

He was positively wringing his hands with his back to me.

"And it's Mr. Beech, you know, Harry Beech. He's a son-of-a-bitch on any day, but after these guys started showing up, he got kinda nice. You know, like he didn't hate us or want to shiv us or something. That's really why we handcuffed him Agent Quinn. We thought he'd shiv us." He was positively vibrating. "He's fuckin' Harry Beech."

So Harry was still tuned into the grapevine, even in protective segregation. Kudos to Harry, but it also spoke to how much power he still held in his hands. I dialed back my skepticism about a sick old man and looked down at the frail figure in the hospital bed. His fearsome hawklike eyes met mine, and then he cocked his head a little to the side.

"What're ya' gonna do about it?"

I thought about it for a full minute. Then I put a hand on Roberto's shoulder and said quietly, "Nothing."

Roberto visibly sagged at the knees and then sighed and left the room. I watched him go and tried to figure out if I'd just made a huge mistake. I could have burned him, and Phillip for that matter, but now if the shit came down,

I'd be in the middle of it too. I sat back down, looked at the floor between my shoes, and wondered what was wrong with me.

"Billy Duggar was my friend, like a brother to me. Always was. This was personal; they're sending a message. You better watch your back Agent Quinn."

He turned his head and brought those eyebrows down.

"You spend too much time with me and they'll come for you too."

Fortress of Family-Harry

At shift change they dimmed the lights in the hallway. Who needs a clock with those two idiots? One comes in; the lights come up. One goes out; the lights go down. Six o'clock a.m and six o'clock p.m.

I was tired. The young FBI agent had tired me out. It's hard to resist him. He's earnest but he's got a hard edge. He might be an okay kind of guy, but I can't trust him. Not yet anyway.

Billy Duggar had been my friend from when we shot marbles in the parkway on Lyndale Avenue. We'd taken first communion together, smoked our first cigarettes together and fucked the same girl—together. As the attrition that is the natural result of bad decisions took its toll on my own family, Billy Duggar had been steady— solid.

Then along came Meredith. An absolute vision of loveliness. Meredith had been out of both of our leagues and we knew it. Luckily, Meredith hadn't, and she glommed onto Billy like her life depended upon it. She asked nothing in exchange save that he abandon his old ways—and old friends. It was a decision that tortured Billy for less than a nanosecond.

The execution of Billy Dugger, and that's what it had been. His execution was a warning. Somebody had sent a message to me and now it was personal. Someone had reached way back, back into ancient history. Somebody with a long memory, someone who knew their history and mine. It was a personal message. I felt bad for Billy and for Meredith. Somebody needs to pay, except I can't do things on my own like I did back in days gone by. Before I'd needed Billy. Now I'm going to need a surrogate— maybe.

A Family Affair

I almost missed the knock. It was almost apologetic, timid, barely loud enough to scratch my consciousness but I'd heard it. Cocking my head to the side, I listened harder, but it didn't come again. I started getting up, but Dutch was already moving to the door.

"Oh my god, Harry, come quick."

Standing just inside the door was my nephew Grant. His clothes dripped onto the mat from the cold spring rain outside, and his lips had turned blue from the chill. Sniffling, he looked at me, then at Dutch and threw himself at me. Wrapping his arms around my waist and burying his face in my chest.

Grant was seven or eight years old; I could never quite keep track. He was a smart kid, tall for his age and skinny.

Right now, he was a scared seven or eight-year-old. I pried him away from me and squatted in front of him. The beginnings of a shiner had started on the left side of his face and eye.

"Hey buddy, what's goin' on?"

"He's come back." He sniffled and wiped his nose on his wet sleeve. "He came back, and I told him we didn't want him to come back. He threw me out and slammed the door."

"He's back? Who's come back?"

His lips trembled and his voice dropped. "Jake."

"How? How's he back? I thought he was gone for good."

"He's come back for mom. Says she has to go with him."

"I thought he was going to leave the country, or at least the state."

"He said he's gotta go and wants mom to go with him. Him and his buddies."

"He's got someone with him?"

"Two or three guys. They stole somethin.'"

"Okay pal, let's get you warmed up and I guess I need to go have a talk with Mr. Jake."

"No Uncle Harry. He said if you show up he'll hurt my mom. He told me he's gonna kill you and Uncle Andy someday."

"Well, we'll just see about that."

By this time Angie had arrived in the front hallway too. I looked at both of them. The look on their faces spoke volumes. Tears were in Angie's eyes.

Dutch looked at me and shook her head. "You should call the police Harry." Dutch was trying to be firm, but she knew I wouldn't do any such thing. "Let's get him in a hot shower and then put him in one of the beds to warm him up."

"Have you had dinner yet Grant?" Angie was catching up too.

"No, I came straight here. I wanted to go to grandpa's but it's too far. Am I ever gonna see my mom again Angie?"

"You bet buddy. Let's get you squared away first though okay?"

I went into the kitchen, picked up the phone, and dialed my brother.

"Hello?"

"It's Harry. Jake's back in town; he's at Kelly's."

"Shit, he doesn't listen very well. How'd you find out?"

"Grant's here, walked all the way in the rain. Geez, must be almost 4 miles and in this weather. Jake's brought a posse with him. Says he's come to take Kelly and skedaddle. He threw Grant out."

"What a douchebag! I'll get my stuff; pick me up?"

"One more thing…"

"What's that?"

"Says he wants you dead buddy."

"Oh yeah? Well like Da says, 'that door swings both ways.' How do ya' want'ta handle it?"

"Guess I'll call Da."

"If you do that, you know what's gonna happen right?"

"Kinda gonna go that way anyway Andy."

Jake Brennan was a nickel-dime criminal from the old neighborhood. A victim of his own fantasies, never quite able to pull off the big score that he could imagine in his head. Either he was a poor planner, enlisted the wrong help, or was just plain stupid. I always leaned him toward the last choice. His main weakness was my sister Kelly Beech, now Kelly Donovan, whom he had adored since they had been in second grade together.

When Kelly married Tom Donovan and gave birth to Grant, Jake had almost lost his mind. When Tom had then been diagnosed with an aggressive cancer and succumbed in just three short months, Jake had thought it was a sign from God that they were to be together forever. The only problem that stood in his way was that Kelly just could not stand him.

Jake's efforts to woo Kelly had become increasingly desperate, and eventually he just resorted to violence. The beatings had gone on for a while, unbeknownst to the rest of us in the family, that is until Kelly had ended up in the Emergency Room. One look at Kelly, with her arm in a sling and bruised face, was all it had taken for my father, Mick Beech, to go dark.

Mick Beech had never been accused of being much of a conversationalist by even the greatest stretch of the imagination, but when he was angry, his quiet demeanor became malevolent. Even as children we knew not to step into his headlights when he was mad. The difference this time, however, was instead of dealing with it quietly and by himself, he stepped back and turned to us.

"You two are gonna handle this."

"Fine with me."

"Me too," Andy's response was only half a second behind my own.

"If I go, I'm gonna kill someone. I don't know how to

be clever about that sort of thing."

"Oh, like I do Da?"

He had just fixed me with that look he was capable of doing, one eyebrow raised and the opposite eye aimed directly at me. He used it whenever I or anyone else said something stupid.

"Okay Da, but I don't want to kill him either."

"Speak for yourself." Andy was hot.

I looked at Kelly sitting in the hospital bed. Her bright blue eyes were red from crying, and the bruise on her face was swelling the left one shut. The look in her eyes was one of fear. Just as we turned to leave the room, my older sister Sally breezed by the nurse.

She took one look at Kelly and turned to Da with a frown.

"Da?"

"Harry and Andy are going to see to it."

"They better—or I will."

It had taken the two of us the better part of the night to find the son-of-a-bitch. It was unfortunate that somehow, in his haste to avoid us, he had managed to fall down an entire flight of stairs—twice.

His luck didn't improve after that either. When he arrived at the hospital by ambulance, he was handcuffed to the gurney by the police officers waiting there for him. He was arrested as soon as he was discharged. Kelly had pressed charges and testified. He was also, curiously enough, found to be in possession of several items of high value which were listed as stolen by the burglary division. They also confiscated an illegal sawed-off shotgun, which I will miss dearly. It had translated into a lengthy vacation down at Marion State Prison with 'three hots and a cot.'

He must have copped a sweet plea deal to be out already, it hadn't been three years since the trial date. Even with time served before he was convicted, he was out early. His arrival at Kelly's tonight was probably one of the dumbest things he could have ever done. There must certainly be a restraining order still in effect, but to risk another traumatic accident like the last one was bordering on incredibly stupid. It also meant he must be planning on moving very quickly.

I picked up Andy at his place. He reached across and punched me in the shoulder, his usual form of greeting for me. He also dropped a set of knuckles into my lap and another set into the pocket of his old fatigue jacket. Together we wheeled across town to my father's house. In the driveway, I looked at Andy. His eyebrows were furrowed, and his hands were clenching and unclenching. Da walked out to the car. He wasn't in a hurry. It was a very familiar walk to both of us, deliberate and heavy with malice. It was a reminder of childhood fear and hard spankings.

We both stepped out and met him at the hood of the car.

"Well?"

"We're gonna go have a talk with him. If we have to chase, we might be gone for a while Da."

"You better goddamn do more than have a talk, Harry."

"Got that right." Andy's voice was tight, angry.

We walked back to the car and I opened the door, but he tapped me on the shoulder and raised a finger.

"Wait here a minute."

He came back in less than a minute, carrying

something hanging by a cord in his hand.

"Here, I made these for you boys. Was supposed to be a surprise, but who knows, might be handy."

He handed one to me and one to Andy.

"What the hell?"

"They're just like mine, but nicer. I used parachute cord and got silver mouthpieces for 'em. They're pretty, don't ya' think?"

By the light of the streetlight, I looked at the one he'd handed me. A cattle horn, over a foot-and-a-half long with a slight curl. The open end had been bronzed and polished; the narrow end was wrapped in fine woven cord with a silver bugle mouthpiece. It was a battle horn and a nice one.

"Blow it."

"What? Here?"

When we were young my father would take his horn into the woods when he took us hunting. He would find a high spot deep in the forest. Once there he would lay his gun down, take off his pack, spread his legs and wind the horn. The blast was so loud in the silence of the woods it would echo through the hills for half a minute and cause the hair on our arms, legs and the backs of our necks to stand straight up. When he did that, his eyes would flame, and he would throw his head back with a great shout blowing the horn again and again until his knees weakened from the effort.

"Blow it."

Andy looked at me and shrugged. He raised it to his lips and gave a blow. The result was a mellow hoot.

"What the fuck was that? I said blow it, not fart into it."

Andy had studied trumpet in grade school and his second effort showed the hours of practice he'd squandered on the instrument; it rattled windows and probably hastened the deliveries of any maternity cases in the neighborhood.

"Holy shit! That is awesome! Wow!"

"Wow's right. We gotta get outta here after that, it's gonna piss somebody off."

"Yep, it's time to go boys. The Beech family's goin' hunting."

"What? I thought you weren't going?"

"I changed my mind."

Kelly and Tom Donovan had bought a small three-bedroom ranch house a little way out of town on a wooded one-acre lot. Tom loved cutting wood and working the yard, and there was enough sun along the south side of the house to have a kitchen garden for Kelly. With Grant's birth, it seemed that their life was on a trajectory of happiness. All that had changed with Tom's illness, and the house had become too much for Kelly to manage with a small boy and left-over hospital bills. We had all pitched in when we could, but the truth had been clear. Without Tom's income and the shortfall of his health insurance, Kelly was deeply in debt and trapped in a house she couldn't afford.

When Jake Brennan arrived on the scene he had at first seemed nice enough. He had paid some of Kelly's bills and wasn't entirely clumsy with household repairs. But that had changed quickly. Kelly still steeped in grief, was not ready or interested in a romance. The fact that she didn't like Jake didn't help either. Soon enough, Jake just resorted to taking his romance by force, and that had precipitated his unfortunate encounter with the staircase.

The steady rain had tapered off to a misty drizzle, and fog had started to rise out of the still-frozen ground of spring. There was no wind, and the drip of water was the only sound in the woods. It was still too early for frogs or crickets to be awake. The house was secluded enough, so it was easier to telephone the neighbors than walk to their house. Once we arrived, we wouldn't be disturbed. As we approached the house on the road, we could see the front door was wide open and the light from inside spilled out into the front yard. Shadows moved in and out of the doorway, and a car sat in the driveway with parking lights on.

"Drive on past and then let me out." Andy was patting his pockets in the back seat.

"Got everything you need?"

"I'm outta cigarettes, got any?"

"No smoking while you're huntin.'" Da was directing the event. "Take the horn, wait until I blow mine then give it a hoot. Got it?"

"Yep, think it'll work."

"It has before."

"What?"

"Never mind, just get out at the edge of the woods, head around to the shed out in back."

"Roger that. Watch your six."

"You too."

I parked the car about a half mile farther down the road in a small lane that disappeared along an old barbed wire fence line and made ready to walk back to the house. The fog was already thick enough so the house back down the road had disappeared.

"You comin'?"

"In a minute."

"Suit yourself. If this goes south, go for the cops Da."

"That'll be the day. I'm needing to think of a way to let Kelly know we're here."

"Pretty sure she's gonna figure it out Da."

"She's probably pretty worried about Grant and scared too."

"I know, it's what I've been thinkin' about too."

I opened the door and stepped out into the lane. I already had my knife strapped to my back pocket and I reached back in to pick up my .38 Ruger.

"No guns tonight boy. Leave it."

I looked up at him in the passenger seat. His face lit by the overhead light of the car. His lips were in a tight line, and his dark eyes flashed. I knew that look all too well.

I left the gun but picked up the horn.

Walking back toward the house, I stayed off the road and on the shoulder. I didn't want to risk a heel strike on the pavement or a stumble over a stone to alert anyone to my presence. The fog would magnify any sound I made. As I neared the house, I heard men's loud voices as they moved in and out of the house, just out of sight in the trees. When I got to the mailbox at the end of the drive, I crouched down and tried to get a count of how many of them there actually were. The sound of my truck starting surprised me, and I swiveled on my heels to see it back out onto the road. Its bright headlights shone through the foggy night as it raced back down the road toward me.

As the truck approached, it braked and swung into the driveway, throwing gravel and fishtailing toward the house. Finally, it slid to a stop in a spray of gravel directly behind the two parked cars and blocked their exit. The driver's side door swung open and my father hit the ground at a dead run directly at the nearest silhouette. Even with his small stature, the collision brought the surprised individual to the ground. Da was immediately astride him and laying into him with both fists.

Two of the other men raced to their partner's aid, dragging Da off and to his feet. The beaten fellow was slow to get up, but once he was on his feet, he immediately gave my father a powerful haymaker to the solar plexus and another left across the jaw. Da slumped, apparently unconscious. The two assistants dragged him to the house and inside. The commotion had all happened within a half-minute and caught me by surprise. In my surprise, I had moved halfway up the lane before realizing that I was out in the open and exposed.

Retreating across the drive and into the brush along the edge of the woods, I hunkered down and looked around. I still needed a census count.

In the house, Mick Beech sat in a kitchen chair and watched the proceedings. His daughter Kelly stood next to him, staunching the blood that seeped from the corner of his mouth. In the living room, Jake Brennan and three other men weighed and separated a large amount of white powder into plastic bags. They were moving quickly, agitated by the arrival of Mick and fueled by the paranoia that a nose full of cocaine brings. They had been in a hurry before but now it seemed that even more haste was called for.

Jake's nose was stuffed full of toilet paper that had begun to turn red. His lip was already puffing up and leaking blood that he continually licked off and his left eye had already started to swell shut.

Mick caught Kelly's hand and stopped it. His hard eyes met her deep blue ones and he smiled up at her.

"It's okay, your Da's here for you now."

"Oh Daddy, you can't be here. You shouldn't be here."

"What? Not come and get you darlin'; these pissants got nothin' to offer that I'm worried about."

"That right you old fucker? How 'bout I shoot a nice 'ound hole in that stubborn 'ead of yours? Think that might make you a little more respectful." Jake's consonants were seriously compromised by his plugged nose.

Mick shook his head and licked his bleeding lip, "A little dipshit like you? It'd take a few more of you than's here tonight."

In two steps Jake crossed the room and slammed his fist down on Mick's left ear.

"Shut the fuck up! You shouldn't've come and now that you did, well that's just a fuckin' shame, cuz we ain't takin' ya' with us. Capiche?"

"I don't speak none of that eye 'talion shit. We'll see who sleeps tonight and where."

"Oh yes. That we will. I only wish I had a couple more of you fuckin' Beech boys here. Man, we'd have graves to dig. Yep, it'd be a shindig. Haha, oh yes we would."

"Maybe they're already here?"

"What? What're you talkin' about?"

"We'll see."

"Shut the fuck up!"

Jake strode to the front, slapping the overhead light

switch off as he passed by. Peering out into the darkness, without the light behind him, he cupped his hands.

"That you out there Andy? How 'bout it Harry, you around? I don't give a shit, do you hear me? Not one god-damned-fucking shit. If'n you guys wanna try and come and get me, there's two of you Beech's in here that will each get a bullet in the noggin' the second I set eyes on either one of ya.'"

There was only silence in answer.

Mick nudged Kelly with his elbow. When she looked at him in horror, he winked and nodded.

"Now m'darlin', now you're gonna see somethin.'"

From outside the unholy two-note blast of the war horn tore through the night.

Inside the house, the four men and one woman froze. Kelly's fingers dug into Mick's shoulder.

"What the heck is that Da?"

"Ssshh now, best you sit on the floor for a bit Missy, here right next to me."

"What the fuck?!" Jake and his voice were completely freaked out. "What the fuck was that? Mick what the fuck?"

"Well my friends, sounds like the posse's arrived." Mick slid out of the chair onto the floor next to Kelly and crossed his arms.

"What the fuck, didn't you guys check the back seat of that truck? Who's out there Mick, is it Harry, or Andy? Don't know which one I'd like to kill more."

"I don't know Jake, never heard any of my kids blow a fuckin' horn like that. Must be somebody else – maybe."

"Trace, get out there and check the truck. Take a gun. If it's a Beech shoot first."

"Why do I haveta' go? I don't wanna fuck with those Beech boys."

"Just shoot 'em. Tony, slip out the back, come down along the side of the house. Keep an eye out and cover Trace. Oh god, if it's a Beech we just about got us a jackpot."

Tony grabbed up a large automatic and headed for the back door. He had just put his hand on the back door handle when another long blast of the battle horn split the night. This time the terrifying sound came from behind the house.

Tony let go of the door handle like it was hot and backed away from it.

"Geezus! What the hell is that noise?"

Another blast of the horn came from the front of the house, and then both were in unison, one in front and one in back.

"We gotta get outta here!"

"Shut up, it's them goddamn Beech's, that's for sure. Nobody else does shit like this. Look at the old fucker, grinnin' from ear-to-ear. You die first motherfucker. You guys start baggin' this shit up. We'll go when I say we go."

Another long blast from the horns, both front and back, layer upon layer of sound that continued for over a minute.

"I don't care! I can't do this! I can't man. I gotta get outta here Jake."

"You go, you don't get no cut. You're out."

"I don't care, I don't wanna find out who's blowin' that horn. I'm gone man."

The terrified druggie went to the front door and flung

it open. With his hands up he stepped out into the darkness.

"Hey! Hey out there! I got my hands up. I'm comin' out. Hey, hey….."

It appeared he had stopped to wait for a response as he paused just outside the door. But slowly, he tipped back on his heels, his head and shoulders reentering the room as he fell slowly at first and then rapidly backward, landing in a sodden unconscious thud on the threshold. A massive bloody wound had appeared over his right eye, and his sightless eyes stared across at Mick and Kelly.

"Rock?" Kelly asked

"Appears so." Mick's calm reply

Again, the horns blew, and again, they blew for over a minute.

"Geezus Jake, who the fuck are these people?"

"That fucker over there's Mick Beech, and those motherfuckers out there are probably Harry and Andy Beech. This slut is his daughter and their sister."

"Fuck me! You mean it's goddam fuckin' Harry Beech?"

"The one and only."

"Man, I don't want to get crosswise with Harry Beech, he'll fuck us all up. I seen it. I seen what he does Jake."

"If it's any consolation to you, Andy's probably worse."

"And they're both out there?" This time he directed the question to Mick.

"Would seem so, yes. I'm afraid you guys are in for a time of it."

"We'll see about that. Get up old man, you and me, we're gonna go out and have a little talk with your boys.

This ends right here, right now."

"Too right." Mick started to push himself up from the floor, but before he could get all the way upright, the lights all went out and the house was pitched into midnight blackness as the power was cut to the entire house. Almost immediately, the horns blew again, and again, and again.

"Don't try anything Mick! I got this bitch by her pretty red hair and I'll cut her ear-ta-ear. Ya' got it?"

Silence

"Did ya hear Mick? Answer me; don't get fuckin' cute with me."

Silence

"I'm givin' you to the count of three Mick, answer me."

Mick's voice spoke from deep in the far corner of the room.

"Boys?"

"Yes Da."

"I'm here too Da."

"Well boys, let's get down to business."

Progress-Thomas Quinn

"What in the name of all that is holy are you doing there if there's nothing to report?"

"Sir, you told me to see if I could get through to him. At least now, he acknowledges that I'm in the room with him. That's progress. Isn't it?"

"By no one's definition is that progress Quinn. That son-of-a-bitch is gonna die, and when he does, he's gonna take all these files down with him. Look…"

He reached into a large file box on the corner of his desk.

"Charles Everly, floater in the Chicago River, C.O.D. strangulation by garotte. Last known associate Harry

Beech."

He dropped it on the desk and grabbed another,

"Mabel DeRoose, dead on a bench at Fullerton Avenue Beech, C.O.D. multiple gunshot wounds. Associates: Harry Beech

He dropped the file and reached into a different box.

"Missing person, Linda Carlson, aged thirty-seven, last seen 09-02-1987, in the company of a tall man believed to be Harry Beech

"Missing person, James Mencorini, aged thirty-seven, last seen 06-28-1989, in the company of Harry Beech at the Purple Onion dance club."

I got two whole boxes of this shit, and the bottom line on every single damn one of them is Harry Beech. So listen up proby, until he dies and is in the ground, you're his shadow. He says one fuckin' thing, you write it down. No more blank reports; Ten-four?"

"Ten four…sir."

A Conversation

The little gnome in the corner wheezed in and out seventeen times per minute for two minutes and sixteen on the third minute. Every wheeze had a characteristic 'click' that separated it from the 'ping' the monitor hanging from the gallows made. Every day was the same as the last one, and the monotony was crushing. I kept reminding myself that this was probably one of the most unique 'stake-outs' that an FBI agent might ever have been asked to perform. But I knew even that wasn't true because some poor bastard had probably pulled or was pulling the same duty in multiple locations. Just my day in the barrel.

I must have dozed off because when he finally said something, I thought I had dreamt it.

"Huh! What?"

"I count every time that boy out there walks by my window."

"Um…yeah?"

"Then I subtract the number of times he looks in through the glass."

"Um…um why?"

"When he goes by and doesn't look, he's going somewhere on purpose. He's got something that needs doing."

"And when he looks in?"

"He's rubberneckin.' Sightseeing."

"Um…so?"

"So Roberto during the day and Phillip at night don't have much to do. There's a lot more sightseein' than there are business opportunities."

I couldn't help myself; he'd kept me waiting for weeks, "They're probably just checking to see if you're dead yet."

"Oh for sure. Jokes on them."

"Me too."

"Oh…did you think we were having a conversation? Wrongo punk, get lost."

"So why do they want you dead?"

"Me? Everybody would breathe a lot easier if they took my name off the dinner menu."

"Like who?"

"Nice try kid. I'm not that easy."

It was the end of another long silent session of sitting and staring at the little blip that ran monotonously across the green screen above his bed. I had memorized every aspect of the room, examined every instrument, peeked in every drawer. I had even considered entertaining myself by practicing picking the locks on the few that were locked. I knew every line on his face and veins in his arms and legs. I put both of my feet back on the floor and stretched. There was no clock in the room, only a hole in the wall with a few wires hanging out of it where one might have been. I had surrendered my watch and other jewelry at the guard's desk, along with my cell phone, so there was no real way to know the time, but it felt like quitting time. As I reached down for my briefcase,

"You ever been shot kid?"

"Yes."

"Where?"

"Iraq."

"No, where on your body dumbass?"

"My legs." In spite of my injuries, I had passed the FBI physical on sheer will.

"Ah, got ya' in the pins."

"Yes. Have...have you ever been shot?"

"Yep, more than once. But I was never shot by the same guy twice. If you know what I mean."

I knew what he meant; it was the same for me. In all this time, he still hadn't opened his eyes.

"Got that tape recorder of yours turned off?"

"I never took it out."

"Then I'll tell you a story about getting shot while I was doing the right thing. You're a cop, so you'll probably love this story. It's about my old friend Frankie."

Frankie

Frank Latoria to be exact. I knew him, but didn't like him. At least not anymore, but I had at one time.

"So now you're the *famous* Harry Beech, eh Harry?"

He wasn't asking; he already knew who I was. He was simply opening the conversation.

"My mother never called me that."

He leaned back in his office chair and took a long pull on his cigarette, holding it in a 3-fingered grip, then blew the smoke toward the ceiling and chuckled while he exhaled.

"Our mother's? Would they? I bet they have some other names for people like you and me, eh Harry?"

I had to admit, Frankie looked good. Really good. He'd probably spent more on his tie than I had on my suit.

The subtle pin-striped suit probably would have been about what a decent down-payment on a new car might have cost. He knew it too; he knew he looked good, and as long as he sat in his chair behind his desk, Frankie knew he was in charge of any meeting to take place in this office.

We were in a large office suite. If I'd known exactly what the word opulent meant, that's what I might have used to describe what the room was like. Frank Latoria was seated behind a huge desk that didn't have one single thing on it except two telephones. One for each hand, I guessed. It was a big desk, but Frank was a big man. The two of them fit together. He was comfortable behind it. So were the two muscle guys sitting uncomfortably close behind me. I leaned back in my seat and met his gaze across all that mahogany.

"Let's leave Mom out of this."

My mother had had two sons. She had learned a long time ago when to roll her eyes and when to look the other way.

"Of course." Frankie relented, "My mother is gone a few years now. She understood how business should be conducted; she stood behind my father when he sat in this chair for a lot of years."

Frank's dad had made his money in Teamster pensions and deal making. His mother, or at least his mother's family, had provided muscle when muscle was the shorter of two routes to a conclusion. When Jimmy Hoffa had taken a dirt nap, the family had suddenly faced less lucrative times. They had moved into the entertainment field and opened nightclubs over most of the Greater Chicago area. Clubs that specialized in recreation of every hedonistic bent a customer may have been interested in. The clubs were popular, and the entertainment was top-notch so a lot of other businesses showed up and set up satellite enterprises. The parking lots were great places where you could find anything you needed. Frankie now specialized in loud music and arranging favors mostly. In the wild times of the late 70s, it was a successful business model.

When Frank took over in the 90s the club's scene began to fade again. AIDS and HIV infections took some of the starch out of his sails and so Frank had branched out again. Now Frank dealt in people; fixing a problem here, arranging a problem somewhere else. On occasion Frank demonstrated a small modicum of conscience, especially if there was money in it for him. He believed in justice as long as it was his kind, and some things he could not tolerate. It was just that kind of problem that Frank had tonight, so Frank had picked up one of his phones, and on this night, that was where I came in.

I had known Frank since we were in 8th grade together. His father had kept a huge cache of Playboy and Penthouse magazines hidden in the ductwork down in their basement. Once Frank discovered them, he and I were destined to be best friends for a while. Then we discovered that we had more than just that as a mutual interest. Pretty soon he and I had combined a tacit nod of approval with a high degree of unsupervised adolescence and the two of us had branched out into chronic school absenteeism and petty criminal activity. Activity that Frankie Latoria had never seemed to get into trouble for.

These activities were doomed by heritage however. I was an Irish-Catholic boy from north of the railroad tracks. Frankie's mother couldn't stand me on sight as a result. And Frank was an Italian-Catholic boy that my mother could not tolerate. Eventually the vocal judgement of the two had won out and we had begun to distance ourselves from each other. But we still smiled and nodded when we passed in the school hallways.

When the 'war' had spawned the draft, I'd had no defense. I'd gone in the first wave and got my shit blown up. Frankie? Frankie took over the family business after his father's unforeseen fatal heart attack.

"You sure about the girl?"

"No question."

"Bona fides?"

"She showed me pictures of her folks. I had it checked out. She's the real deal alright."

"Is it a problem?"

"No man," he lit another cigarette and waved the smoke away, "she wants to go home. Serious."

"Okay, so why do you need a courier Frankie? Just call the old man, cash the check."

"There's the rub old friend. She's got a boyfriend; my cousin." He squinted one eye, "he's not part of the program."

"Oh?"

"He says she goes over his dead body. Geez Harry, she's fifteen years old."

"So?"

"So, he's twenty-seven or twenty-eight. He's pumpin' that thing couple times a day, but she's gonna get older. The guys a fucking pervert pedophile, but he's my cousin. That takes it outta my hands Harry, you know how it is," he shrugged his shoulders, "It's outta my hands," he looked across the desk and raised an eyebrow, "but it ain't outta' my reach."

"So?"

"So, take her home Harry."

"How much?"

"Half."

"Nope."

"Sixty-forty."

"This cousin? He hooked up?"

"Sort of."

"Sort of?"

"Yes."

"Then nope."

"C'mon Harry you're the pro at this stuff, everybody knows that. He won't fuck with you. C'mon…for old times' sake? She's just a kid, she's scared and she wants to go home. He's got her strung out on 'god knows' what. She needs to get a chance."

He opened a drawer and crushed out his cigarette in an invisible ashtray.

"Seventy-thirty and Bob and Tony walk you out with her." He said finally.

"Where is she now?"

"A couple of the girls are keeping an eye on her back in the dressing room. She can't be seen within a hundred miles of this place. I'd lose my liquor license. Go through that way, and you can go out the side door." He handed me a small slip of paper with the particulars on it. "Where are you parked?"

"Handicapped space right outside the front door."

"Oh, how do you get away with that?" He shrugged, "Give Bob your keys and have him pull around to the side.”

“No thanks, I’ll go get it and meet you by the door with the girl. I want ta’ look at this *cousin* of yours straight on—on my way out. Be nice if one of your girls could keep him busy for a few minutes after that.”

“Can’t. He doesn’t like any of my girls; they’re all too old for him. He’ll be okay. By now he’s so coked up he doesn’t know his ass from a hole in the ground.”

“Great a coked-up junkie, with a personal agenda. Great! Next time call somebody else for stuff like this Frankie.”

“C’mon Harry, everybody knows you’re the best. I have to call you when I got stuff like this. Wait until you see this kid, man; she’s all that and a box of chocolates.”

“She’s fifteen.”

“She’s still good lookin’,” he fixed me with a no-nonsense look, “no matter how old she is.”

I flipped my car key ring and caught it in my other hand.

“Have her at the door—ten minutes.”

“Ten minutes, should take you five max.”

“Ten minutes.”

Bob, the bodyman, pointed out the ‘cousin’ on the way to the front entrance. Sure, I knew him. Some pissant kid, Johnny or Jimmy something-or-other, probably six or seven years younger than me and Frankie. We’d used him as an errand boy back in the day. Now he was a fat, sloppy drunk, slouched down in the pleather booth, a drink in one hand and a smoke in the other. When he saw me though, he sat straight up, and his eyes darted to the door that led to Frankie’s office.

It was going to take more like fifteen minutes.

It was early summer, and the parking lot was still bright enough so that the lot lights hadn't taken full effect yet. The lot was filled with people moving around, smoking and leaning on fenders on an easy summer evening. Girls watching girls, boys watching girls; the usual. The cars parked at the edge of the lot where weed was still king were doing a brisk business, and a thick cloud of smoke hung in the air above their heads.

On my second lap of the lot, he stepped into my headlights. He was quicker than I had expected. I would have guessed maybe third or fourth lap. When I stopped he slammed his fists on the hood of the car and yelled,

"What're ya' doin' here Harry? Get the fuck outta' here."

He had the attention of every single person in the lot, and the entourage that had followed him out. He had my attention too, but for a different reason: he was scratching the paint on my hood with all his jewelry. I swung one foot out of the car and shut the door as casually as I could. He was in my face almost before I turned to face him. A little spit was hanging out of the corner of his mouth. Isn't it funny that it's such a vivid memory? He was drooling a little, all the while cussing and swearing and yelling at me.

My first kick landed full-on in his groin; it was a real two-fer. He went down on his knees and grabbed his crotch so I helped him back to his feet again. Once I had him leaning against the car and breathing raggedly, I asked him, "What's her name?"

"*Cough…cough…*what? Who?"

"Guess."

"Who? You mean that cute little piece of ass."

My second knee kick dropped him on the pavement again, but I'm anything if I'm not a gentleman, so I helped him back up to his feet—again. Now his nose was running, and he was sniveling.

"What is her name?"

"Um…Melinda…or Mandy…um…"

My third kick left him curled in a ball on the pavement.

I drove around to the side door, where Tony was peeking through a small open crack of the security door. I hopped out and pulled the door open. He shoved a semi-conscious girl in Daisy Dukes and a peasant blouse into my arms and pulled the door shut. In a few seconds, she was sprawled across the back seat of my car and I was almost ready to go.

"Hey Harry!"

I turned toward him, just as the pistol in his hand went off. It wasn't the first time I'd been shot, but I make it a rule not to be shot by the same person twice. As soon as the gun had gone off, the parking lot full of people scattered like chickens in a rain storm.

Jimmy Something-or-other, no Mencorini, yep that was his name Jimmy Mencorini, little pissant.

I don't know what Jimmy had been expecting. Maybe some version of 'Oh no! I'm shot, oh dear.' But that's not what he got. Mandy was sprawled in the back seat, so Jimmy went in the trunk. It wasn't until the next morning that I finally got the bullet dug out.

I kept 'em you know, the bullets. Had 'em in a jar on my dresser. Good reminder sometimes when you're getting ready for a job. You give that jar a shake, it makes you humble—makes you careful.

Not Good Enough

"Goddammit Quinn! We already know that Jimmy Mencorini was last seen with Beech.

"The fact that Harry admits that he had an altercation with him is public knowledge. There were at least twenty or thirty eye-witnesses, but we still don't know what happened to him after that. Shit, for all we know he's bussing tables at some upscale restaurant in British Columbia. Where did Mencorini end up? Beech knows that and when this is over, I want you to know it too. Did he tell you anything else?"

"He told me that Jimmy shot him."

"No shit? So he killed him in self-defense?"

"No sir."

"Well at least you've got him talking. Keep it up, and

find out what happened to Mencorini for starters. I can give you a few names to ask him about if you want a list?"

"Maybe later, but right now I think I should just see if he wants to tell stories—maybe."

"Stories? I don't need stories; I can get those a dime a dozen. Get me some evidence, and make it snappy. Doctors don't know why he's even still alive. By all accounts we should have missed this opportunity completely. Go make friends with him, or see what makes him tick, what's keepin' him alive. Find out what he wants and then, by God, give it to him. I don't care what it is. Make him want to talk to you Quinn."

Bad Dreams

I struggled to the surface in a sweat-soaked frenzy, fighting my way up through tangled bed sheets. My small studio apartment was dark, darker than usual, and my sleep-clouded eyes couldn't seem to adjust. Sitting up, I swung my legs onto the floor and tried to piece together the shreds of why I'd woken in such a state of confusion in a room where I could barely see my hand in front of my face. Reaching out, I pulled the small chain on the bedside lamp, but the light did not come on.

The power was out. That explained the darkness. The whole block must have been out because there was no ambient light. No light pouring in through the windows from below, no street lights. It was late enough so that no headlights passed in the street below. The silent dark world of after midnight dread.

A blinding flash of lightning suddenly lit the two windows at the end of the room, the flash so intensely bright that it seemed right outside—only feet away. Reflexively, I threw my hands over my ears and dropped back down onto the damp pillow waiting for the thunder. But even before it arrived another flash, also impossibly bright, lit the room in stark silhouettes of black and white. Then the thunder arrived, and I cringed, trying to make myself as small as possible. Pushing myself across the bed, I braced my back against the wall and clutched the pillow to my chest. Unbidden, tears filled my eyes and beyond reason, I sobbed as the thunder rattled the loose glass panes of the old windows.

It was an instantaneous transition, the flashes, the great pounding thunder. The flashes of lightning lighted a different landscape behind my tightly closed eyes. I couldn't help it; I felt the world tilt away from me and I slid. I slid down and into the abyss of my secret hell. My eternal shame in a scenery lit in photographic snapshots of black and white. Razor wire stretched across my vision, grimy faces, eyes wide with the terror of the moment. Another flash, a body where a boy had been standing in the last flash. The earth trembling with the explosions, the rattle of automatic weapons, the storm raged inside of me while the storm raged outside against the apartment windows. In the thunder of the storm I again heard the screams of men in desperation, '*Mayday, mayday, mayday, we have incoming, mayday, mayday, mayday!*' '*Ammo, ammo here*! And finally, "**MEDIC, MEDIC** over here **MEDIC!**" "*Ammo, ammo, ammo!*", "**MEDIC!**"

For fifteen minutes the storm outside poured down its fury. The windblown rainwater sheeting off the windows in wavy torrents and splashing on the sills below. For those fifteen minutes, I stared blindly into my past. It didn't happen every time, but when it did, the paralyzing dread rendered me weak and vulnerable. It was fifteen minutes of 'wrong place, wrong time' in my past. Fifteen minutes, it is said, is such a short time in a man's life, only a moment really. It only takes a moment to change the course of someone's life.

Just fifteen minutes, but an eternity of sensory overload. Afghanistan, the wind whipping the sand in a frenzy of static electricity, visibility almost zero. But still they came, and we fought back; the 173rd Airborne Brigade lost at least one man for every one-half-hour, day after endless day. The sky was filled with static discharge, flashing lightning and crashing thunder in tinder-dry air. The thunder roared down on us from on high, and when it did, it brought mortars and rockets with it—and death. We couldn't find our ammo in the mirk, we couldn't find each other in the wind whipped landscape, and most of all, we couldn't find the dead as they were buried in the blinding sand.

"You ever been shot kid?" He'd asked.

I hadn't even known it happened. I only noticed later, after the storm had passed.

Sally Carlisle

The gate guard had insisted on calling ahead once I'd shown my shield. Now I was trudging up a long curving driveway to a very nice house where a woman stood on the top step with her hands on her hips and scowl on her face. It wasn't just a nice house; it was a seriously nice house on a seriously quiet cul-de-sac in a seriously nice neighborhood, and it was the nicest house on the block.

"Is he dead?" She asked before I reached the bottom step.

"Harry? No ma'am."

She cocked her head to one side, "Atta boy Harry."

"I was hoping to speak with you Mrs. Carlisle, if you have a moment or two?" I held my badge up for her to see it.

"Are you kidding?" She looked down at the little picture behind its plastic protector, then she raised her gaze and looked at me at the foot of the steps; her eyebrows rose, her jaw tightened and the smile faded. "I've got lots of moments, nothing but moments; around here there's plenty of moments."

"Beg pardon?"

"A bird in a gilded cage, Special Agent Thomas Quinn. Look across the street and look down the street. You've attracted the Homeowners' Association. They're on full alert. What is it that you want?"

Across the street a man had stepped out on his front porch and stood gazing across the street with his arms folded on his chest. Two lots down the street at the inlet of the cul-de-sac, a minivan sat at the curb, a man in sunglasses was seated in the front seat.

"I'm sorry ma'am. I had no idea."

"Don't call me ma'am please, I'm old enough but I still don't like it. Come on in…damage is done already. Might as well see if it was worth it."

Once I was on the porch, she held the door open and gestured me in ahead of her. Inside the entry was brightly lit in soft off-white pastels. A long staircase ran up the right side of the hallway and the walls displayed tasteful and probably expensive artwork. A small sitting room opened to the left. Instead of directing me into the sitting room, she led the way down the bright hallway and into a large open kitchen.

"So, you're here about Harry." She wasn't asking. "Is this a cup of coffee conversation or a glass of wine conversation?"

"I was wondering about Jimmy Mencorini."

"Oh my! It's a martini conversation—excellent."

She lifted down a martini glass out of a beautiful rack of hanging glasses and began busying herself with a martini shaker. "Are you on duty Special Agent Quinn or will you join me?"

"I'm technically not on duty, but I'm not much of a martini guy, ma'am."

"Coffee? How about a beer? And please stop that. Call me Sally; that's who I am and who I used to be."

I looked at her as she mixed and shook the martini in the shaker. There was a file on her downtown too, just a little farther back in the drawer from the Harold Beech file. Sally Beech, a.k.a. Sally Carlisle, alias Sally Square. There weren't any bad angles; she was strikingly lovely. Past middle age, but barely or at least seemed so. Athletically thin, dressed in a loose blouse that must be silk and matching off-white slacks with stylish tan flats she gracefully moved about the room. Her hair was perfect, and unlike most women her age, she had let it go grey. This woman gave aging a very good name. I knew what her age was; it was in her file, but I would have guessed at least fifteen years younger looking at her. Finally, she slid a counter stool around to my side of the counter and straddled it with a deep sigh. Her new martini poised in one hand, and she handed me a bottle of beer.

"What about Jimmy?"

"Well, like what happened to him?"

"I don't know. If you guys don't know, who does?" She took a long sip.

"He shot Harry."

"Yes he did." She took another long sip, "But not twice."

"Harry said the same thing."

"Harry always said that. It was like his mantra." She spread her fingers in the air. "You could fool him, lie to him, even shoot him and you might get away with it, but you weren't going to get away with it twice."

"So, what did he do to Jimmy?"

"I don't know. You'd be surprised, but you're not the first person to ask me what happened to Jimmy," another sip, "or a dozen other people."

"I'm sorry. I'm not trying to intrude. There's just something about Harry. I met him once when I was a little kid. He was bigger than life back then. Everybody wanted to be Harry Beech when we played cops and robbers."

"Really? How did you meet Harry?"

"It wasn't a big deal but I was running errands for the men at the Italian American Club on Fullerton back in the old neighborhood. Harry came out and gave me ten bucks to run to the corner and get him some smokes. He told me to keep the change."

"That's funny, I wonder why?" She forgot about her glass and massaged her forearm for a moment. "Ya' don't say; Harry didn't smoke. I'm his sister; I'm pretty sure I never saw him smoke."

"That's the weird part. When I got back with his cigarettes, he was gone. I never got a chance to give them to him. There wasn't anybody on the sidewalk, so I tried to give them to the guy at the door. He told me Harry Beech wasn't there and hadn't been there that night. He smacked me on both ears just to emphasize his point. I got the message, so I never told anybody about it."

"Curious," she sipped her drink and looked critically at me, "But what do you think about it now? Now that you've got all that trained FBI paranoia under your belt?"

"I don't know, never thought about it much." I looked at her and she cocked one eyebrow. "He was trying to get me away. Something was going down?"

She saluted me with her glass and eyed me over its lip while taking another sip.

"Smart that boy is, no witnesses and go out the front door when you can, but remember the way out the back just in case. How long have you been a 'feebee'?"

"I graduated from Quantico the first of October."

She whistled through her teeth, "Four months and they threw you into the deep end with a shark."

She got up, paced to the window, and looked out into the backyard.

"Harry took good care of me. This house, the neighborhood, the lifestyle. He and I were eventually all we had, just he and I. The rest are all gone now, but Harry and I were always the closest, and when we were growing up, we took care of the others. Even after the others came, it was Andy, Harry and I. That is before it all went to hell, and then…" She looked across at me, "…and then, after Andy, then it was just me and Harry. Like in the very beginning, just me and Harry trying to get by."

She shrugged, "Harry is easily the smartest man I have ever met," she smiled back over her shoulder, "and I've known a few men in my life. He could charm the pants off anyone and get comfortable in a room with assholes or anybody else in it. By the time he left, every one of them would believe they had a brand new and most excellent friend. But not Harry; he didn't make friends, and he had no friends. He would not let nor could he make himself trust anyone. He was incredibly intelligent but seemed incapable of emotion, maybe with only one or two exceptions. I sometimes wonder if he ever even trusted me.

"Women? Gracious but how they loved Harry. He might have had some amazing bedroom skills in addition, but his real forte was how he treated them. He treated them all like queens. He was respectful, attentive, kind and completely genuine. He honestly just loved women, all women and they loved him right back in return. They couldn't get enough of him. Harry needed a new car, voila a new car. Harry needed a place to stay, voila how about a month in St. Thomas. It was like that for Harry. They didn't even seem to mind that there were as many of them as a few at a time. Harry could look you in the eye and tell you the sky was green, and even though you knew it wasn't, you wanted it to be."

"Sounds rough." I smiled at her

"But when he got shot, he called his big sister, not one of them." She tossed down the rest of the martini and finished in a hard voice.

"Mencorini got the message, but some people are just better listeners than others."

I had momentarily lost myself in her narrative; when she slammed me back into reality it took a few moments to reorient myself. I tried to focus and not fantasize about what I wanted to hear. I let her go without interruption and geared myself to just listen.

She was a fascinating conversationalist. Through two more martinis, she talked about the old times, the hardscrabble times down 'behind the yards. She talked about everything and nothing, more lonely and conversation starved than a star witness.

Finally, when the light was tilting in the kitchen window she began to wind down and I rose to leave.

"Would you like to stay for dinner?"

"No thank you Sally; the Homeowners' Association already has enough to worry about."

"By now, they're not worried. They probably know your blood type and who your maternal grandparents were. Harry is holding a lot of secrets, and some of them shouldn't see the light of day. There are people that want it to stay that way Special Agent Quinn, so be careful." Then she smiled and put a hand on her cocked hip. "And come see me again sometime."

When I walked back down the driveway, the 'across-the-street' neighbor stepped down off his front porch and strolled down to the curb next to his mailbox. His arms were still folded on his chest, and there was no sign of a welcoming smile on his face. He didn't say a word but silently watched while I got in the car and started the engine. Instead of turning around in the next driveway to leave, I executed a perfect three-point turn, turning directly at him. I was within a foot of him when I stopped before reversing and he never twitched, but as I drove away, he calmly raised his right hand and gave me the finger.

Bobby Dey-Dey

The sun broke the horizon over my left shoulder as I drove south on I-55. I had one hundred miles in the rearview mirror already and another two hundred plus to go. I rubbed my eyes and took a long hit out of my mug of cold coffee. I had hoped to be farther along before the light came up. When you drive south in Illinois, it's best if you do it in the dark. The farther south you go, the flatter it gets. Miles upon miles upon miles of corn fields in the summer and barren moonscape in the winter, all the way twenty miles to the horizon in every direction. Nothing to look at except the mile markers and nothing to think about except how long it took to get to the next marker.

In the last several miles, the radio station had petered out to static. I was tired of the morning drivel of local radio, so I hadn't bothered to look for a new one. The agency car performed well enough but lacked all the most basic creature comforts: heater, air conditioner, AM-FM radio. Instead of looking for a new station, I shut it off, bumped up the cruise control a few more miles per hour, and thought about Harry Beech.

In the last few days, Harry had begun to speak to me. In the first few visits, he hadn't even acknowledged my presence. Then it seemed he had accepted it at least, but grudgingly. Finally, I admitted to him that I had visited his sister and he had opened an actual conversation. He was anxious it appeared, to hear about his sister and how she was getting along, what if anything she might need. He expressed himself in surprisingly philosophical observations. I found myself shocked, almost half expecting that a mass murderer would not be able to have ideas of a philosophical nature. My training and my street experience had warned me that most criminals had above average intelligence but it was surprising to speak to one who expressed himself so clearly.

One thing was clear: Harry's weakness was Sally Square.

"How's the old girl look?" He didn't even try to veil his interest.

"Like a million dollars."

"That's Sally, always the looker. Even way back, she could snap her fingers and the boys came running. She could have had any one of them if she wanted, but instead she settled on the weakest link, little Tim Carlisle. Never understood what she saw in him." His hands danced around under the bed sheet, "Oh he was handsome alright, in a sort of future vagrancy sort of way, but a dreamer;

couldn't keep a job. Or wouldn't. Jobs were never challenging enough or paid enough." Harry shrugged, "Always an excuse. What he liked was sports betting and what he was good at was lying on the couch."

This was more like a conversation than had come out of Harry at all, let alone in one burst, so I pressed my luck. I already knew the answer to the question; it was all in the files, but I had to ask it anyway. I had a feeling it might be a good question.

"What happened to him?"

"Car accident, killed." He sniffed and looked away. "Suspicious circumstances."

The FBI file on my desk said the same thing, '*Suspicious circumstances.*'

"I'm sorry for Sally." I tried to sound appropriately contrite.

"Nobody else was." He huffed. "There were plenty of people would have been glad to escort Tim out the exit. Me for one. He owed big time on his bets and hocked everything Sally had worked to get. Most of all, everybody just loved Sally, so they were ready to hate him. Most of them snarled and raised their hackles when discussing Tim Carlisle. And if it hadn't been for Sally, there's no telling what would have happened to him."

"Must have been rough for you to watch."

"How's that song go? '*If you knew Susie, like I know Susie,*' well I knew Sally. I knew she'd take it until she wasn't going to take it anymore. Then she'd more than likely kill him herself. I left it alone."

"But others didn't maybe?"

"Bobby Dey-Dey had a particular hard-on for Tim Carlisle. Partly because Tim married Sally and partly because Tim owed him a lot of money." Harry shrugged his emaciated shoulders. "Bobby ran a chop shop down on the south side. After the accident, I always kind of wondered about it. If Bobby might have done something to the car. He had a temper with a real short fuse and he knew cars inside and out. I didn't like Tim any better than the next man, but hey, he was my brother-in-law." He looked far away to a seemingly distant memory. "Bobby's doing fifteen to twenty down at Marion last I heard."

So now I was on my way downstate to Marion Federal Penitentiary, where one Robert James Dey, aka, Bobby Dey-Dey, was putting in his time. Bobby had been caught in a sting selling untaxed cigarettes and cigars off the back of a truck. Business had been good and Bobby had made quite a reputation for himself. Unfortunately, when the sting went down so had a couple of law enforcement people. As a result, Bobby had gotten a few extra years tacked onto his sentence. Now he had eight in, and he'd been a very good boy. The police officers had recovered and he had been working in the laundry and taking college classes in the library. So now he was up for parole.

I had caught a break, my first one since almost never, he was up for parole and it looked like they would probably let Bobby go. But there was a fly in the ointment. Bobby, suddenly didn't want to get out; he had rescinded his parole request and no one knew why.

At the prison, I showed them my shield and surrendered my sidearm. I had called ahead and made the arrangements with 'the powers that be.' Bobby Dey-Dey was expecting me but when they frog-walked him into the conference room in handcuffs with the long chain, I was surprised. He was supposedly up for parole. The precautions seemed a little over the top. But then I took a good look at Bobby.

Bobby Dey-Dey had stayed in shape, and Bobby was a very big guy. His hair was shot with grey, long and shaggy across impressively wide shoulders. *'Bobby Dey-Dey ran a chop shop down on the south side.'* His posture was ramrod straight, and he walked with a wide legged stride that was only half the result of the leg shackles, but also the effect of very tight leg and thigh muscles. Bobby worked out and it showed.

The fun ended there. His face told a different story altogether. His eyes were wild, and he had a twitch in the right one, making him blink like somebody's yard light getting ready to burn out. The guard pushed him down in the chair and then fastened the chain to a ring bolted to the floor. I slid my chair closer to the table he was sitting at and said my hello's.

"Who da fuck are you?"

"I told you, I'm Special Agent Thomas Quinn."

"No dumbass. Who ***the fuck*** are you? What're you doin' here?"

"Same question, same answer."

"Are you gonna help me out? Is that what you're doin'? Comin' down all this way?"

"I heard you're up for parole. You're due."

"Fuck that man, I ain't goin' nowhere."

"The parole board might not agree."

"Don't you see?" He licked his lips and looked over his shoulder at the guard, then leaned forward and whispered, "Don't you know nothin' man?"

"Nope. Pretty sure I don't know what you mean."

"C'mon man! Everybody knows. That's why I gotta stay in here. I gotta watch my ass, it's about to get hot! I can't get out now, shit, I won't last on the street more'n a week, maybe two. There's too much at stake."

"In here you mean?"

"Everywhere man, everywhere. Shit don't you know?" He put both hands on the table and leaned across, meeting my eyes with a furrowed brow. "Harry Beech is dyin'!"

"Who's Harry Beech?"

"Oh man, are you for real!?!"

"No seriously, who's Harry Beech?"

"What are you doin' here man?" Bobby slumped back and waved his arms in the air in disgust rattling the chained cuffs. "You ain't gonna help me. Shit I'm a dead man either way."

"I'm here for something else. I just wanted to ask you about something that I was following up on. I just stay in my own lane."

"The fuck? What? What could you peckerheads think of to ask me after all this time that you haven't asked me a hundred times already?"

"Bet this is a new one."

"Yeah? Try me."

"What really happened to Tim Carlisle?"

Bobby's eyes got really big, and he slammed his fists on the table and he pulled the floor chain tight. The guard moved forward but I waved him back. Just the same I slid my chair back a foot or so.

"Who gives a rosy rat's ass what happened to that little pissant."

"Well apparently, there's been a little research done

lately and it turns out that the insurance company might want all the accidental death benefit back that they paid his wife, Mrs. Sally Carlisle. Something about a fire that started after the initial accident and was the apparent cause of death."

"Where the hell…? What? You're FBI. Why are you even involved?"

"Inter-agency cooperation. ATF, your friends if I remember correctly, asked if we'd look into it for them."

"So the fire was suspicious? Now? After all this time, shit it's like ten years ago."

"I'm new, so I get the stupid shit details. They sent me all the way down here to ask if you might know anything about Mr. Carlisle's death or if he may have been involved in your illegal tax stamp business."

"I wouldn't have trusted that son-of-a-bitch with my laundry."

"So 'no'?"

"Wait." He held up his hand in a stop sign. "Wait. What if there was like something else? You know, like a possible other cause of the accident that explained the fire or something like that. Would Sally still keep the dough?"

"Pretty sure." (What did I know?)

"If like something sort of 'caused' the accident? Sally still keeps the money."

"As long as the aggrieved widow didn't participate in any wrongful doings, I would certainly think so."

Robert Dey put his elbows on the table and steepled his fingers. He looked at the wall behind me long and hard.

"One way or the other, today, tomorrow, or next year, Harry Beech is gonna die. Whether you know him or not,

Harry's gonna die. When Harry dies an entire library is gonna burn down and everything he knew will go with him. Maybe. Word is he's talking to the feds. If that's true, when he dies, the bets will be off. The people that were friends won't be anymore, and the people who were already enemies, the gloves come off. Harry kept it all inside and when he dies all the agreements are dissolved. It's the rest of us, the ones that knew him, you know, worked for him. They'll come for us. All of us. Harry was the barricade; he never let anything past him, but that's all gonna be over. It's not the best place, but at least I can watch my back in here."

He stood up and signaled to the guard to step over. When he did, he looked up at him through his long hair.

"I would like to confess to the murder of Timothy Carlisle."

Special Agent In Charge (SAC)

"Well you're a real whiz kid Quinn, congratulations. Now you're closing cases that weren't even open."

SAC Wilson rocked back in his desk chair and looked down his chest at me. The station chief had taken the news about Robert Dey's confession with skepticism and a wry smile.

"It's hard to close any case, so when we do, whether it's ours or not and whether it was by accident or not, we toast and then get back to work. Good job Quinn, your instincts are good. This time they paid off. This is gonna tie up Dey-Dey's parole hearing in the courts for a while while they get it all sorted out."

There was going to be more once these formalities were out of the way. The SAC was just warming me up. He had something else he was working up to.

"What did you think he meant Tom? About the trouble when Beech dies?"

"I don't know. He said that for people that were already enemies, the gloves would come off."

"Think for a minute Tom. There are seventeen open FBI files where this guy has implicated culpability. And that's just the FBI cases. This guy knows where every single body is buried. Shit, it probably wasn't just cars that Bobby Dey-Dey was crushing down at that junkyard of his.

"Harry Beech was the fixer, the cleaner up of messes. He kept his peace and had people on both sides of the aisle. Everybody trusted Harry Beech with their innermost secrets and do you know why?"

"Why?"

He looked hard across the desk at me. "Because he kept them."

"I got that, but once he dies. It's like Bobby Dey-Dey said, the library burns down. Nothing but ashes left; the secrets go when Harry goes."

"Wouldn't that be nice."

"It's something different than that?"

Dan Wilson rocked forward again. With a grin he reached forward and picked up the stapler from his desk. Gesturing with it he said, "Let's say Mr. Stapler here has a problem. Not an easy problem, certainly an inconvenient one. He knows the solution he wants, but doesn't know exactly how to get it done. He's not that kind of guy."

Setting the stapler down he reached over and picked

up the pencil cup next to his desk lamp.

"Mr. Pencil Cup has a specific skill set. He would be ideal to help solve Mr. Stapler's difficulty but alas, his loyalty and attention are focused in a different direction. He is not opposed to a little freelance work, but has difficulty making friends outside of his small circle."

He reached into his shirt pocket and brought out a small butane lighter.

"Mr. Lighter here is a professional listener." He waved the lighter back and forth, "He learns of Mr. Stapler's difficulty; he is also well acquainted with Pencil Cup's skill set. Mr. Lighter facilitates a meeting, then a negotiation, and finally the inevitable conclusion, whatever that may be. Both participants are well satisfied. Mr. Stapler is relieved of his *problem*, Mr. Pencil Cup has a special payday, without involving his current employer who may or may not have approved his freelance activities. Both happy, both with a secret, and the keeper of that secret is Mr. Lighter. Both forever in his debt, both tethered to him by their mutual secret. So then, sadly Mr. Lighter passes away." He dropped the lighter back into his shirt pocket, "and the leverage those secrets represented evaporates.

"All over the place people will look around and wonder who knows what, who remembers what. They'll be on uneven footing. They'll need new alliances, new friends and a whole new batch of secrets to create. There's gonna be a lot of pushing and shoving. Believe me, they're already starting to consolidate in preparation. Just look at page four of the Tribune every morning. The jockeying for position is already underway."

He rolled forward and put his elbows on the desktop.

"So far so good Tom, but I got a call from the MCC (Metropolitan Correctional Center); they're amputating Beech's left leg in the morning. Something about his systems shutting down or other. Anyway, no visiting tomorrow. He'll be in recovery most of the day. The time is getting shorter and shorter; you've gotta up your game a little. Take those files back to your desk and study up on them some more. There's got to be a way into this guy's good graces. You gotta make a new friend."

He rolled back in his chair and shook a cigarette out of the pack on his desk. Before he lit it with Mr. Lighter, he added, "And do it quick. Pretty soon, there's not gonna be much of Harry left.

"Also, you're due at the range, so study up and then brush up. Shooting a few magazines of parabellums always makes me feel good. I understand you're a pretty good shot."

"Isn't everybody in this job?"

"You'd be surprised."

Post Op MCC

On the upside, I'd finally met Phillip, the night nurse/orderly. On the downside, I had been sitting in the plastic chair so long that I was in danger of having my ass cheeks fuse to it. I'd sat there long enough watching the beeps and blips hanging from the gallows behind his bed that I'd matched their rhythm to popular songs in my head. I'd even given a bass line to the little white robot in the corner who breathed in and out on the third downbeat like a clock. Turns out they were all sad, slow-dance numbers though. Through it all Harry Beech hadn't moved, moaned or flinched. I would have liked to say he looked like death, but didn't want to remind myself that I knew what death looked like.

Finally, I stood up and stretched, pulling my slacks

and boxers out of my butt crack.

"What're you doin' here?" His words were almost a whisper, but his consonants were still strong.

"Thought I'd see how the surgery went."

He gave a small snort, "Bullshit. You wanted to make sure I wasn't dead yet."

"You look like it."

"Get lost punk." He had never opened his eyes, but now his head lolled to one side.

I sat back down in my ass-clenching chair. I had no place else to go and nothing special waiting for me anywhere either. I was starting to think this was more interesting than it should have been. I wanted Harry to talk to me. I wanted to hear his story, even if I was doing it in my spare time.

Time passed and I must have dozed off because when I opened my eyes, he was staring right at me. His hawk-like eyes were lucid, and his brow was pulled down tight. Despite myself, I flinched and sat up straighter.

"Okay, so are you here again, or are you still here from before?"

"Still here."

"You think I'm gonna die and you don't want to miss the fun."

"That's not it."

"You want me to give you some dirt, maybe fall on somebody. In my grief at my impending doom, I'll try and make peace with my maker by making someone else's life as miserable as mine. Or maybe I'm so sedated that I forget to watch my mouth and maybe blurt out some tasty little tidbits of information."

"No." I looked down at the floor, "I've got no place to

go and all day to get there. You're probably the most interesting person I've met so far in this job."

"So now I'm overcome with emotion at that confession."

"I just wanted you to know. It's interesting. I don't read much, and I don't have a television."

"Take up drinking then. And get lost kid."

"Okay, I give up. But Mr. Beech, please, can I ask you a question? Just one, and I've waited a long time to ask it."

"I got the time."

"Why'd you do it? Way back, I was at the Italian-American Club. You gave me ten bucks to go down and buy you a pack of cigarettes. 'Keep the change,' you said. It was the most money I'd ever had that was mine. When I got back you were gone. I kept the change, and I smoked the cigarettes, but why did you do it?"

His mouth clamped tight and his lips drew a straight line. If possible, his eyebrows came down farther and he stared straight ahead for a full minute. Then he looked back at me.

"I remember that."

"So why'd you do it?"

He looked back at me under those eyebrows and then looked at the wall for a long minute. Then he looked back at me and said, "There are many hallways in memory. Each lined with filing cabinets of our past. Events both real and imagined. Some are dusty from neglect and forgetfulness, and some are visited regularly. When the heart is restless, it is the dusty cabinets it seeks, and often the contents prove difficult to read.

"That's a direct quote. I memorized it. Guy named

Michael Nelson. That's where I go these days. To the dusty cabinets like the one you just opened for me." He gave me a hard look and then looked back at the glass wall. "Kid…have you ever heard of the legend of Baba Yaga?"

Baba Yaga

"You mean, like, the boogie man?"

"Yes, in a way." He paused and took a few deep breaths, then he looked out through the glass, "The Baba Yaga is an enigmatic witch. Real but not real. But usually we think of her as vengeful and evil, but she, or it, was also a cleanser of evil, a righter of wrongs, a merciless enforcer.

"When you've been around long enough to see the whole story. Not just the outcome or the chapter you happened to come in on but the whole story. Then you see the justice or the lack of it in most situations for what it really is. You participate in the specific event, but you also see who wins and who loses overall, not just who wins this round or that round, but overall. What's the long-range benefit or loss, what pieces will be used and what pieces sacrificed? The ones that win are not always the ones on the side of right, but everyone defends their positions with a very self-righteous zeal. Those are the ones that are the hardest to forget, the self-righteous ones that were on the wrong side of justice but won anyway."

"So?"

"So, sometimes it's necessary to level the board. Sometimes when the bad guy keeps winning, the questions of right and wrong get a little cloudy. When that situation is created then it becomes necessary to do the right thing even if it's technically the wrong thing or there's no justice. And there are people that do that. The Baba Yaga's of the world. Individuals who will do a job and not question the morality or ramifications of good and bad. They take the job, do the job and don't think about it again."

"So what does that have to do with a pack of cigarettes?"

He looked at me for a long time before he answered. When he did, you could see the tension in his shoulders raise them slightly, and he took more than one deep breath.

"If you used to hang around the Italian-American club, then you probably knew who Charlie Halliday was."

He made it sound halfway like a question and halfway to see if I really had been hanging around the Club.

"Sure. He was a dude. Snappy dresser. Tipped us good to watch his car. Always had a nice car."

"Exactly. Good time Charlie. Maybe the original Good Time Charlie even. Everybody knew Charlie. But not everybody liked Charlie."

"Everybody seemed to like him."

"Charlie was a good guy. WWII vet. Decorated multiple times. Came home got a good job. Entry level. But in the right place at the right time. He went to work as a trucker, but in no time he was tagged to be part of the union brass. Not high level, but on a more important level, if you know what I mean."

"No, I don't know what you mean."

"Money. Money boy, the stuff that makes the world go round. Money. The big shots do all the talking at the Union Hall, but the money guys, those guys, they make it happen or they make it not happen. Charlie Halliday became the money guy."

"I didn't see Mr. Halliday that night at the Club."

"That's because he was never there."

"I don't understand."

"Charlie was getting a 'little long in the tooth' as they say. He'd been around for a while and he'd greased a few palms. But Charlie didn't only handle the money; Charlie liked money personally. Charlie had started making friends with people who had money to give him in exchange for favors. The Teamsters, at that time, were for sale and Hoffa was selling, and it needed to stop. Charlie sounded the alarm. He told anybody who would listen to him that the Teamster's pension fund had sprung a leak. Hoffa was in prison at the time, but he was still pulling the strings. Charlie wanted them to catch Jimmy at his game, but it backfired. Some of it was legit, but some of it was Charlie. When the counting took place, there were going to be a lot of questions, and Charlie wasn't going to have a lot of answers. He was given a warning; then he was given another. He didn't listen. He thought he was untouchable."

"He wasn't?"

"Nobody is kid."

"So? Charlie took the money and ran?"

"You see, Chicago teamsters had always managed their own affairs. Just like Philly and the East Coast did. Sure they voted as a block when it came down to it, but the local business stayed local.

"Then there started to be money coming in from Vegas. Money and muscle. The Teamster pension fund was big and fat and Vegas was growing fast. It needed more money to make it grow even faster; politicians needed to be paid off, contractors, lots of open palms to be greased. They were building a city where nothing like it had existed before. People were taking a lot of interest in our Chicago business and whispering into a lot of ears. Those ears listened to all the voices and union members started not to listen quite so much to the union leadership. Jimmy Hoffa was on shaky ground after he got jailed and Charlie was in the middle of that, right in the middle. He was pushing the Vegas agenda and showing those Vegas guys where and who to spend money on. So that was why he got warned."

"But he didn't listen—apparently."

"No he didn't. The money was too good. Instead he doubled down."

"Doubled down?"

"Charlie went to Hoffa."

"Oh."

"Oh is right."

"What happened? Did he make a deal?"

"Jimmy Hoffa was a lot of things, but most of all, he

was his own man. Jimmy never let anybody tell him what to do or when to do it. Most of all, if there was going to be a deal, any deal, Jimmy was going to make it, not some two-bit, Chicago bean counter. On the surface he laughed it off, but on the side, he told the Chicago boys to handle their own shit."

"Talking to Charlie wasn't working, so what did they do?"

"That's where your pack of cigarettes came in. That night Charlie got to go for a ride."

"So? He learned his lesson? They beat a little sense into him—right?"

"Probably."

"Probably?"

"I never saw him again."

"But . . .did he just disappear? What happened to him?"

"No one knows what happens when Baba Yaga comes for you."

He frowned and winced when he tried to move his newly missing leg.

"That night Baba Yaga came for Charlie Halliday, and nobody else needed to see it." He looked back at me and met my eye. "The night Jimmy Hoffa got his way."

"But you know what happened to him."

"Hoffa? Nope, not for an instant. The Vegas boys were tough. Tougher than we were ready for and they got the pension, and they got Jimmy Hoffa and Charlie Halliday would have won. No I don't know about Jimmy, but just between us and the world, we know what happened to Jimmy. And now you know what happened to Charlie, even though I don't actually know. And you know how I know stuff like that?"

For the first time I saw a smile on the face of Harry Beech. I would be glad to wait a long time before I saw another one.

"Who do you think shakes hands with the Baba Yaga?"

Who Shakes the Hand?

"Charlie Halliday! Shit, haven't heard that name in a while"

The Chief rocked back in his creaky office chair, put his hands behind his head, and looked up at the ceiling.

"Before my time, but I remember it. Sure, the Bookkeeper, that's what they called him. Stuff of legends some of that stuff is, but I remember the Bookkeeper."

Then he dropped his arms, leaned forward and put his feet back on the floor. His eyes drilled a hole in my forehead.

"Why?"

"Well what about him? Was he famous or something? Did something happen to him?"

It was Monday morning and I had paced my

apartment the entire weekend thinking about what Harry had told me about Charlie 'The Bookkeeper' Halliday. I decided to shortcut a bunch of research and go straight to the library. Dan Wilson was the master of all cases open and shut, and my curiosity was boiling over.

"Don't bullshit a bullshitter Quinn. Harry gave it up."

"Okay."

"What did he say?"

"Who was this 'Bookkeeper' guy anyway?"

"Not as famous as Frank Wilson, but probably more important."

"So who was Frank Wilson?" The Chief could spend another ten minutes warming up to his subject and then another thirty telling it. The 'ants in my pants' were in a hurry this morning and adding more characters was just going to make it take even longer.

"He was the accountant that took Al Capone down. Excellent detective work, diligent, meticulous even, but he got the results and put Capone away. That kind of stuff is why I joined the Bureau. Grind 'em out, do the work, get results."

"So—Halliday?"

"Halliday wasn't an accountant. In fact, he was out of his league really when it came to accounting practices, but he didn't need it. He was a planner, and he ran all the little bean counters that did know accounting practices. Halliday was a street fighter. He had hard-knuckled his way into the leadership of the Teamster's Union here in Chicago. He was sharp and vocal. He wasn't shy about stating his opinion and the newspapers printed most of it."

"So he pissed people off."

"Exactly. Charlie Halliday envisioned the potential

and clout that kind of money had in the Teamster's pension fund. He was an investor, just not with his own money. He wanted the leadership to advance into the twentieth century and he had a plan. There were politicians and law enforcement who were ripe for bribery, and Charlie wanted to buy them. It was the Charlie Halliday plan and he shouted it from the rooftops."

"How do you know this stuff?"

"I studied when I was at Quantico. That's why you're there." He tipped his head back and looked down his nose, "Didn't you?"

"I passed my exams."

"Tsk tsk." He gave me a 'disappointed' look and then continued, now at last truly warming up to his subject.

"Jimmy Hoffa was a lot of things and you don't get where he got by being a creampuff. Jimmy had his own ideas about the pension fund. He was heavily invested in mob connections here, the East Coast, and, most especially, Vegas. He'd made his promises and got the deal he wanted. He didn't want to listen to Charlie. Shit Charlie was making his life difficult on a daily basis from the way I read it."

Dan Wilson reached in a desk drawer and pulled out a pack of cigarettes, shook one out and lit it with the lighter from his shirt pocket.

"So what then?"

"So, then Charlie took a flyer. Right outta' the blue, he disappears." He took a long hit off his cigarette and blew the smoke at the light fixture, "disappears along with a cool million-and-a-half."

"He stole the pension?"

"Not hardly. There were millions and millions at stake, but he disappeared and so did a very tidy 'retirement' bonus. Shit, a million-and-a-half, that'd be worth ten, maybe twelve million in today's dollars. I wouldn't mind getting my hands on that myself. It was a 'missing person' and also involved possible 'Interstate Commerce' issues so the FBI looked into it and concluded that he had just disappeared."

Dan Wilson leaned back in his chair again and pointed his cigarette at me. There was no fooling him; he knew where I got the question from.

"So what did Harry tell you about Charlie Halliday?"

"He said he never showed up for a meeting, and then he never showed up anywhere else after that either."

"And didn't he find that curious?"

"He didn't say that he did."

Special Agent in Charge Daniel Wilson cocked his head to one side and raised his eyebrows, "He didn't say that he did." His voice was almost incredulous.

"No, instead he was talking about Baba Yaga. He kinda like *implied* that he knew this Baba Yaga personally."

Dan Wilson rocked forward in a shot and slammed both hands on his desk.

"Goddammit, if Harry Beech says he knows Baba Yaga personally, you believe him by God! What else? Did he say anything else?"

"No."

"NO? Nothing?"

"Just that he can shake hands with him."

"Jesus! That's it?"

"Then he asked me to leave so he could take a nap."

"Jesus! We need more Quinn. You've got to lean in on this guy. Get more specific, study the files. You gotta scratch his itch." He ran his hand over the prematurely balding scalp and rolled his eyes, "Charlie-by god-Halliday—Jesus!"

Sipping Whiskey

I stopped at a local Walgreens and bought a cheap bouquet of flowers. Expensive to me, cheap to most people's taste. I wasn't going in empty-handed this time and this time I had been invited—sort of. When I pulled up to the gate the guard took his sweet time coming out to the car, almost a full five minutes. Once he did, he gave me and my back seat a quick scan and then we played 'twenty questions' for another five minutes before he waved me through. I was willing to bet he didn't give the Amazon or UPS drivers that much trouble.

Rounding the curve leading into the cul-de-sac, the across-the-street neighbor was already out examining his ornamental foliage. It was a cold day and he was in short sleeves so I knew he'd just stepped outside after a phone call from the guard shack. This time instead of parking on the street and walking up, I pulled up her driveway and avoided the meaningful glare he aimed in my direction.

Sally Carlisle met me at the top of the porch steps and smiled when she saw the flowers.

"Ooh Detective," she simpered, "you must be trying to butter me up for a big favor!"

"No ma'am, just being polite."

"What did I tell you about calling me that? It's Sally." She grabbed my elbow instead of the flowers. "Well c'mon in. I'm freezin' my ass off out here."

We hustled in the door, breezed past the sitting room and foyer without pause, and made our way down the hall to the spacious kitchen. Sally pointed to my previous seat and held her hand out for my coat. She hung it on a hook inside the back door and spun back into the room where she whisked around the center island and reached down two glasses. It was barely twelve o'clock in the afternoon, but she started to hum while she collected things and mixings. I gave myself a gentle reminder to go easy as I settled onto my stool at the end of the counter.

"It's Saturday. So I know you're not officially on duty, and I need to hear a little news of the world. So Detective —you're my entertainment for the afternoon."

"Sally I'm not much of a martini man."

"Whiskey it is then!"

She wheeled around and quickly replaced the vodka bottle in the freezer. Spinning on her heel she turned to a beautifully carved wooden cabinet against the wall.

"Let me see, let me see."

She opened the cabinet to reveal shelves upon shelves of bottles in all shapes and sizes, all glad to see the light of day.

"Irish? Scotch? American? Hmm? Tennessee or Kentucky? Maybe Virginia?" Her voice was almost reverent, "What's your pleasure Detective? What's your poison?"

There were too many choices and I said so. She reached in and brought out an expensive-looking bottle and showed it to me.

"Got some of the sipping variety here. Blanton's; you'll like it. Runs a few hundred bucks a bottle."

She poured two snifters of whiskey and twirled them before handing one to me. I tasted mine and it evaporated before I could swallow it. It was love at first taste. Sally smiled and dropped down on her forearms from across the counter. Fingering the rim of her glass, she asked in a seemingly nonchalant manner.

"How's Harry?"

"They amputated his leg last week."

"I heard. What a shame. Harry was a legendary dancer. What a shame."

"A dancer?"

"You betcha.' Harry knew how to move his feet. He was not really a nightclub kind of guy, but, in those days, that's where the business was conducted. Harry was a good dancer but a better listener." She touched a sip to her mouth, "Harry was always the guy in the corner booth."

"Well, I'm afraid those dancing days are over. How'd you hear about it? Does the prison or jail notify next of kin?"

She slouched down in her seat a little. "I'd be stunned if I was listed as next of kin."

"But how'd you hear about it."

"Get real Detective, you know how the world goes around. Word travels faster than the speed of light." She leaned down and gave me a hard look. "I heard."

"Sorry Sally. I didn't mean to really question it; I was only curious."

"Curious can be dangerous unless you get paid to be curious. You're not on the clock, not on duty," she paused with her glass and cocked a shoulder and with a sly look, "so why are we so curious on a Saturday, Detective?"

"Why do you call me that? I'm not a detective; I'm FBI."

"Still a detective, and still here to question me." She smiled a million-dollar smile, "Aren't you?" She swept away from the counter, "Although the flowers are nice. Thank you. A girl likes that once in a while."

She took a long sip of her drink, and then waving the Walgreen's bouquet, lifted down a small vase and began arranging the flowers in it.

"Harry have anything to say?" She said casually.

I tried to assess whether her interest was feigned.

"No. Not lately anyway."

"Was he talkative before?"

"No, practically never."

"Practically?"

I couldn't help myself, I'd backed myself up into a conversational corner. I had let my guard down and thought I was having a normal social dialog; instead, I'd run right through a 'STOP' sign.

"I learned about Bobby Dey-Dey."

"That dipshit?" She didn't pause in her arranging, "So what?"

I mentally wrung my hands. Shit! I'd stepped right

into the middle and now I was about to make it so much worse.

"He's confessed to the murder of your husband."

"You don't say! Well that is news." She stopped arranging the sparse flower spray. "Anything else?"

"Not really. Harry's mostly verbally abusive, to be honest."

She chuckled and sat back down on the counter stool.

"Well then, that probably means he likes you." She tilted her head back and took a deep swallow of the divine libation. "No, I meant anything else about Bobby and my dear departed husband?"

I took the next ten minutes relating everything I could remember about my visit down to Marion State Penitentiary and my encounter with Bobby Dey-Dey.

"Well, well, well. Bobby Dey-Dey, no kidding, I owe him a huge debt of gratitude." She raised her glass to the room. "Thank you, thank you, thank you, Bobby Dey-Dey."

I'm sure I looked a little puzzled, which she noted.

"My beloved husband has been gone more than a few years now. He was a putz; worse, he was a putz's putz. He was gonna get it one way or another. Believe me, he more than paved that road. Sooner or later he was gonna get it. So, now I know who to thank."

I took another sip of the whiskey and worked it around in my mouth, trying to extract every last bit of the flavor from it before swallowing it while she continued.

"Look I loved him; god knows I loved him, in spite of who he was. He just sounded some kind of bell inside of me. He wasn't a good man, I knew that all along but I just couldn't resist him. He was like kryptonite for me. I loved and hated him, but I couldn't leave him and I couldn't stay. But man, I loved him in spite of it all."

"Do you really think he did it? Bobby Dey-Dey?"

"Plenty of people wanted to. Bobby knew his way around cars. Jeez, he had a sweet ride back in the day. '57 Chevy with a Hurst transmission and posi-traction, baby blue two-tone." She sloshed the tumbler and shivered. "Bobby was a pretty boy. All looks no substance. Oh you know the kind, on the fringe, never gonna be a roller, but always gonna be the roller's best friend. Never gonna hit the homerun, but damn sure gonna be happy with the singles, doubles and maybe a few triples." She shrugged, "that was Bobby Dey-Dey."

She reached across the counter and pulled her purse to her. Reaching in she fished out a pack of cigarettes and a small turquoise lighter. After shaking out a cigarette, she turned toward the open end of the room and lit it. Taking three long puffs and directing the smoke toward the skylight, she turned and put the rest of it out in a saucer on the counter. Reaching out she lifted her snifter, emptied it and set it carefully back on the counter. She raised her vision and addressed me across the counter.

"I'm sorry. That's a lot to process all at once."

"I can imagine. I'm sorry. I kind of blurted it out, I know I should have tried to couch a little better way."

"No, it's okay, honestly I appreciate it."

"No, I should have just kept it to myself."

"Nonsense, detective. It is just that now I've got some issues of my own because of it."

"What do you mean?"

"Now I've got to deal with my own conscience."

She refilled her snifter and took another long swallow.

"What? What conscience?"

"Mine."

"Yours?"

"I'm the one who turned Bobby Dey-Dey in, in the first place."

Charlie-by god-Halliday

Sally stood up and strolled the kitchen perimeter, then stood with her back to me looking out the windows over the sink. She put her hands on her hips and stretched her back. The winter sunlight streaming in backlit her silhouette, making gossamer out of her tasteful outfit.

I took a long sip of my whiskey and tried not to stare too obviously.

"I must be getting old; it's getting harder and harder to remember who I owe an apology too anymore."

"I guess we start collecting those right from the start. I know I've got a couple."

"A couple? Wait until you're all grown up Detective. There's an apology owed for every decision you make. Someone gets their way, someone doesn't. Apologies accrue.”

“You sound like you collect them.”

“You should be careful there Tom Quinn. Piling one owed apology on another eventually turns into favors owed. That’s where the trouble starts when you owe a favor, and it’s tied to an apology that you also owe.”

“So what’s the solution.”

“Don’t fuck anybody over. Easy-peezy.”

She sat back down at the end of the counter space, picked up her glass, noticed it was empty and picked up the bottle instead. After refilling her own glass, she one-handedly slid the bottle the entire length of the counter toward me.

“But don’t get fucked over either.” She added and took another long drink. Then twisted a lock of her perfect hair and looked coyly across at me.

“So is that it? You just happened by to drop that little tidbit today, or was there something else? Hopefully, a little more socially appropriate perhaps? Maybe a little more—fun?”

“Not really, I didn’t really come with the express intent of dropping that bombshell on you, but I thought you would want to know about it. Bobby was pretty terrified of getting his parole. He said that with Harry gone, he might be in some kind of trouble.”

“Harry has a lot of secrets. Lots of leverage. I can’t imagine what Bobby would be worried about, but if it’s so important that he’d go down for another twenty, it must have been a big issue. At least to Bobby anyway.” She looked up at the far corner of the ceiling and, with a small smile, said, “My goodness, what else could he have been up to down at the auto yard that he doesn’t want anyone to know about? Sounds like Bobby's got a few secrets of his own to worry about."

Somehow my whiskey glass had emptied itself during the exchange. Sally pointed at the bottle and waved her hand. I took the hint and with my glass in my hand again, I looked a question at her.

"But the secrets die when Harry does. So I'm lost."

"Remember what I just said. Apologies become favors. Favors pile up. Everyone owed Harry favors, or apologies—or both.

"Harry did favors for people. It was his profession. What if you do something heinous? Maybe you do something a little or a lot illegal. You need to cover it up, make the scene appear normal. You'll need some help but that help has to be trustworthy and professional. You get the help because you know a guy. You get away with it, but now someone else knows your secret. There are always two people in every exchange, good or bad, the fucker and the fuckee. What happens when the guy that helped the fucker dies and now the fuckee wants his money back, or worse, his life back? What if the only reason he hasn't come for it before is because of a favor owed or a promise kept? What happens when they all want their little piece of the sky back and want it all at once and the only thing keeping them from it is the promise or favor owed to a dead man?"

"Shit!"

"Shit is right. That's what is likely to happen, except that nobody knows what anybody else is thinking—or wanting. But we're gonna find out pretty soon now."

"He sure is a tough guy."

"There's tougher, but I've never met them. Harry

could be hard when he needed to be." She looked away for a long moment, then nodded slightly and took a drink with a shrug. Then with a smile that could launch ships, she asked.

"So, anything else? Harry have anything else to share?"

"Not really, we talked about Charlie Halliday."

The change in her expression was instantaneous. One second she was soft and warm; in the next a curtain dropped over her face. The smile she still held had gone cold, and her eyes tightened. In the next second she caught herself and looked away.

"Charlie Halliday? What's the Bookkeeper got to do with anything?"

"He said he was there the night Mr. Halliday disappeared."

"You don't say?" She waved her glass at me but didn't make eye contact.

"That's all, just that he was there but not that he knows what happened to him. He's legally dead now, but it was a missing person's case before that. I looked it up."

"Do tell."

"I was just curious, you know, because of what you and I had talked about the last time I was here. The pack of cigarettes thing."

"That was that night? What an amazing coincidence." She emptied her glass again got up, walked around to my side of the counter where the bottle was and poured another healthy splash. After another swallow, she strolled back to her seat, running her finger along the countertop. "His disappearance made quite a few headlines. He stole a lot of money before he left town I heard."

"About a million-and-a-half."

"That'll get you a nice start somewhere else. Good for Charlie. Maybe he'll turn up in Venezuela one of these days."

"It's been a long time; I sort of doubt it."

"Me too." She raised her glass toward me. "To Charlie Halliday," and we both took another drink. "I met Mr. Halliday way back then. I wasn't too impressed."

"What!?"

"Charlie Halliday liked the ladies. I was a lady. Well sort of a lady."

"Did you know him?"

"Knew he was a clod. All knuckles but no 'know-how.' No manners, just talk. Thought money was going to buy him some class." She finished, took another drink, and looked past me. "It didn't. Anything else?"

"About what?"

"Did Harry have anything else to say?"

"No. Well he told me a story about the Baba Yaga."

"You're kidding? What in the world for?"

"He wanted me to know that he knew Baba Yaga personally."

She smiled a sly cat's smile.

"What?"

"You can count on that one." She looked down into her glass. "If Harry Beech tells you that he knows the devil himself," she looked up, met my gaze and finished in a serious voice, "then you should believe him."

So? What Do ya' Think?

"So, what do ya' think?"

The SAC was on the edge of his seat. His elbows were on the desk, and for once he wasn't doing two things at once. I had his full attention.

"Think? What do I think?"

I had gone to the SAC first thing in the morning. It was a week since I'd sat in his office and told him about my interview with Sally Square. It wasn't a Monday or Friday when assignments were turned in or handed out. It was supposed to be just another day for him, coffee and a cigarette, maybe a phone call or two. He wasn't expecting me or my energized state. I arrived at the office early, early for the staff and especially early for me, in fact, but not too early for him it seemed. I had spent the night before pacing the floor, staring down at the street below from my apartment windows, and most importantly, not sleeping.

I was not sleeping for what I thought was a very good reason, and I wanted my SAC to be a part of it. I was not sleeping because I had visitors the night before. They had not been the spirits of Christmas past, present or future. But like the fairytale, they had tried and succeeded in their endeavor to scare the living shit out of me. They had been friends of Harry Beech—or so they said.

<hr>

I had circled for blocks before I found an unprotected parking place along the curb. It had snowed on and off for three days and parking spaces were coveted and protected commodities. In Chicago, people had been shot for taking someone else's parking spot. The one I found was a three-block walk home, but it was a godsend just the same. The Christmas lights on the city streets dominated every storefront and every street light pole. Christmas trees winked and blinked from upstairs walk-up apartments above the storefronts and snow mounds dominated the curbside between street and sidewalk. Sidewalks were wet with grimy slush and it splashed beneath the tires of passing traffic.

It was well into late afternoon darkness by the time I got to my apartment, and my shoes and socks were wet through. The entrance to my apartment was sandwiched between a shoe repair shop and a take-out pizza joint. The latter being my usual dinnertime go-to. The narrow entrance was a doorway between the two storefronts, and it opened into a small alcove before a rising staircase rose to the four small studio apartments on the second floor. Inside, the alcove sheltered the four mailboxes for the apartments and a scattering of sale flyers and ancient newspapers on the floor below them. There was a single bulb that lit both the alcove and the staircase.

Seated on the staircase was a man who filled all the rest of the available space. He stood up when I opened my mailbox and stepped down into the alcove with me. Because of the size of the alcove, he was immediately too close to me.

"You Quinn?"

"Sorry?"

"You Quinn?"

I recover faster than I used to, but it still took me a moment.

"Depends. Who wants to know?"

"Me."

"Who's me?"

"I'm Jackie."

"Do I owe you an apology or something?"

"We wanna talk with you."

"Who's we? And what about?"

"Let's talk."

And with that he turned around and started up the stairs. I stood at the bottom of the steps and watched him retreat into the semi-darkness. Eventually he disappeared around the corner. Then I heard a door open and close.

I hurried up the stairs and then hesitated at the door of my apartment. If he was in my apartment, that would be breaking and entering. He hadn't appeared to be the least bit friendly, so I considered going back downstairs and calling the police. Technically, I could arrest him but he was almost twice my size. He was inside my apartment, and he had said, "We".

My bills were being paid mostly and I was reasonably certain that my student loan broker didn't send muscle when my payment was late, so I was a little curious but not stupid. I drew my sidearm before I turned the knob and pushed open the door.

Every light that I owned and some I rented were on. The place was aglow in light. Tall, dark and loathsome from the alcove downstairs stood at the front of the room leaning on one of the two window sills. I had one chair that fit under my small kitchen table and it was occupied by a guy who was a look-alike to the first guy. Sitting on my unmade bed was an older gentleman dressed in a three-piece suit. He stood up when the door swung all the way open.

"I apologize for this intrusion Agent Quinn." He signaled to the troglodyte sitting at the table to move. The second giant rose and joined his buddy on the other unoccupied window sill. "Please sit down; I am here as a friend. I just wish to speak with you as a friend about a certain matter which may be of some importance to both of us."

I was on edge, standing there with my Glock in my right hand, facing the overly full room and ready to jump right out of my skin.

"Seriously Mr. Quinn." His tone was even and modulated, smooth. "I mean you no harm and I do apologize for this intrusion, but I felt that a little discretion would be better served. I have some information that you might be happy to receive."

I made eye contact with him but didn't lower my gun.

"It is in regard to your current investigation. Perhaps bad news, maybe good news."

"You are in my apartment. You've broken into my apartment. I have no idea who you are. And you're here to give me some news?"

"Yes."

"You expect me to lower my weapon?"

"Under similar circumstances, I might be leery as well. But all I can do is assure you that I have information that you would like to have. I also have a message for you that you should hear."

"Says you."

"Boys please leave us." He looked back over his shoulder, "Go down to the car. I'll be down in a minute or two. Agent Quinn won't shoot me if you two leave us alone, I believe."

The two hulks looked at each other, then at the old guy, who nodded. I backed up into the kitchenette and let them pass as they exited. Their heavy shoes echoed as they went down the old wooden steps to the street. The old man sat down on the empty kitchen chair and sighed.

"My name is Joseph Battaglia." He rubbed his eyes, "I am an old friend of Mr. Harry Beech. I mourn the state he is now, and I remember what an incredibly vital individual he was. I believe he still may be. You and I should have an understanding about that first and foremost."

I hadn't chambered a round in the Glock at the outset and now I ruefully laid it on the bed but within easy reach. Unless this guy was a third-degree ninja, I was pretty sure I could take him in a fair fight. There wasn't anything left for me except to take a seat on the side of my unmade bed and lean forward. Either the room was awfully hot, or I was sweating for no reason at all.

"You are younger than I expected."

"Sorry to disappoint you."

"No. That isn't a good thing or a bad thing. I had assumed that someone of Harry's reputation would garner a more senior agent."

"Well Harry's not exactly terrific conversation."

"So? You are speaking with him?"

"I visit him a few times a week. Speaking with him isn't the same thing."

"But he has not refused to see you."

"No." I hadn't really considered that he might do that.

"So you are establishing a rapport."

"NO! Not at all. Mr. Beech is not entirely friendly. And what we do talk about is none of your business."

"I trust Harry. He wouldn't say or tell you or anyone else something that he didn't want to. You've been seeing him now for almost a month. He has never denied you access, in spite of a strict no-visitor policy. Anything Harry might tell you should be considered important."

He reached into his inner pocket and drew out a thick cigar.

"Do you mind if I smoke?"

"It's against my lease."

"I'll speak to your landlord."

He drew out an ornate lighter and burned the end of the cigar, slowly rotating it and taking his time.

"You would be interested to know that they transported Robert Dey, Bobby Dey-Dey, to Chicago so that he could be arraigned on charges of the first-degree murder of Timothy Carlisle."

"Why didn't they just do a video arraignment?" I couldn't help myself. This guy knew more than I did.

"He asked to do it in person. A chance for a road trip after years of incarceration, I don't know, but they brought him to Chicago."

"Okay."

"He was attacked as he passed down one of the hallways heading to the lockup. Stabbed multiple times. He is dead, I'm afraid." He took a long draw on the cigar. "Unfortunate."

"What!? Where was the guard?"

"He was temporarily called away to a security issue."

"He's dead?"

"Yes." He took a long drag on the cigar and exhaled, casually making eye contact with the ceiling. "I thought that due to your involvement with him earlier, you would like to know."

"How do you know about this?"

"That is unimportant. It is a fact however. No one is entirely safe, as they say." He drew on his cigar again and rose from his seat. Walking to the windows, he exhaled and then spoke with his back to the room. "You are becoming friendly with Mrs. Carlisle."

"I wouldn't say friendly, but we have spoken. Once again, that's none of your business."

"What is or isn't my business is up to me…and some others."

He turned around and sat on the window sill, flicking ashes into his open palm. I had to turn on the bed to maintain eye contact with him.

"Harry is a very sick old man. He was my friend, but he will be leaving soon. Life goes on for the living. There are doors that should remain closed. Stories that should remain untold. People deserve to live their lives without someone knocking on their door or bringing up the past. No good thing can come from the work that you are doing Mr. Quinn.”

“I have a job to do, and it was given to me whether I liked it or not. Whether I like it or not, I’m going to try and do it.”

“Yes, that is what a good policeman should say.”

“Well I’m trying to be a good policeman.”

“But my warning has teeth in it.” He rose and paced forward, “Bobby Dey-Dey should have taken the parole, but he was confused.”

“He seemed pretty sincere to me.”

“I’m sure he was, but he made a mistake. He thought that his story was more important than all the other little stories. He lost the thread of importance.”

“So…so what is the thread of importance that I shouldn’t miss?”

“I’m not here to threaten you Agent Quinn. I’m actually here as a friend, both to you and to Harry. I have a message for you, and I think you should consider it seriously.”

The cigar was starting to fill the room with smoke and my eyes were starting to smart. I stood up and faced him across the narrow space.

“What’s the message?”

“Leave it alone. Harry’s not going to give you anything. Just leave it alone.”

“That’s not much of a message.”

He put his cigar out in the used saucer on my kitchen table, his other hand casually in his pants pocket. “For what it's worth." Then he walked to the open door and, with one hand on the doorknob said, "And stay away from Sally Square. I will be in touch."

<hr>

"So what do you think?" The SAC was still sitting forward, his forgotten and unlit cigarette between his fingers.

"I think I need to spend a little more time with Harry."

"That's certainly what I'd do."

"And maybe with Sally Carlisle too."

"Why?" He was confused.

"If I'm not supposed to bother her, it means I'm bothering someone else. There's gotta be a reason anyone cares."

"I doubt it. I'd concentrate on Harry. Sally Square's nothing to nobody anymore."

"I'll confine it to my off-duty hours if it bothers you."

"Goddamn! Are you getting a hard-on for that old lady? Don't do that Tom."

"I'm not, but she is a very interesting person, and she might be able to find a way to tweak Harry. Besides, she's not *that* old."

"It's your investigation. But hurry it up."

Popsicle Diplomacy

I hadn't had as much trouble with it as I thought I might. Mostly I got shrugs and raised eyebrows. To say the least everything was thoroughly examined and inspected but I hadn't broken the seal on the package and it looked innocent enough, even if it was a completely futile effort.

When Phillip let me into his room, he was awake and the stare leveled at me seemed ambivalent. I didn't get the usual scowl or what might have been worse; he didn't try and ignore me. Instead, he watched me steadily as I put my things on the chair. What I'd had little trouble getting past the gate guard was a small igloo cooler that I'd picked up in the jail cafeteria. The fact that it came from their own cafeteria was probably what had finally gotten it past the guard.

I opened it and took out an entire box of orange popsicles which I showed to Harry.

"I've been reading up on your condition." I said, "It said that one of the problems people faced when they've been treated for cancer was that their salivary glands kind of stop working. They can't make enough spit anymore. That's one of the reasons that the patients say they can't taste anything anymore, and their mouths are too dry. So, they lose interest in eating. I thought you might like to try one of these?"

"No thanks," he whispered, "but I appreciate it Agent Quinn. You're trying that's for sure."

"Oh come on, I had a hell of a time getting them to give me the cooler. Just maybe humor me? You know, you're not the most fun person to spend time with, and honestly, I'm just trying to do something nice this time."

"Well shit. Okay, give me one."

I opened the box and took one out. After I slid the wrapper off, I broke it in half and wound the wrapper around the stick, then handed it to him.

"Geez, that's cold," he rasped. "Hurts my teeth."

I took my usual seat and watched as he devoured the thing in seconds.

"Give me the other half."

Once he got the second one, he slowed down and spent time savoring the sweet and icy thing. He didn't speak or make eye contact. He just sat and looked into the distance while he rolled each small bite around in his mouth.

"Got any cherry?"

"Nope only orange. Had enough trouble getting this

in."

"Well thanks."

I almost blushed.

"So…if you're trying to bribe me, it won't work, but you've managed to improve my mood some. That's good for a change. For that I may be open to a little conversation. Give me another one of those first though."

I was glad he was a little more open, but I had intended to question him tonight one way or the other.

"I had a visitor yesterday. In my apartment."

"Do tell." He wasn't looking at me as he slowly drew on the popsicle.

"Joseph Battaglia. He said he was a friend of yours."

"Joe Battaglia," he held the popsicle out at arm's length, examining it, "*was* a friend of mine."

"Was?"

"Personal." He was giving serious attention to the popsicle, "What did Mr. Battaglia have to say? I bet he's worried that I might be spilling his beans."

"That came up."

"I bet. Well, no worries there."

"He told me Bobby Dey-Dey got capped."

"Yeah. Happened a couple days ago. Right here in this house." He finished the popsicle and held the stick up for examination. When I offered the second half, he shook his head. "No it's making me a little sick."

"He told me to 'leave it alone.'"

"I'm sure that's what a lot of people would tell you. I'm a little surprised that I haven't been capped myself to tell you the truth."

"Well he made it pretty clear that he'd be visiting regularly, especially if I keep coming to see you. Trouble is Harry, this is my assignment. I don't really have a choice.

I'm detailed to sit in this fucking chair whether you tell me anything or not. It's a shitty job but it's my job, so I brought you popsicles. I didn't bring you popsicles because I'm trying to butter you up. I thought it would be a nice thing to do, and I thought it would be fun to watch you enjoy them. If you hadn't wanted them, I would have been just as good one way or the other."

"That's quite a speech. You mean it?"

"Mostly."

"Fair enough."

"He said I was too young for the assignment. Kinda' hurt my feelings a little."

That got a smile out of him. He looked at me still with a smile.

"You're daddy was Michael Quinn, Mickey Quinn wasn't he?"

I recoiled a little. My father had never come up in the conversation, any conversation. My father had been a good man, solid, a good provider who had mastered minding his own business long before he met me.

"Yes, how do you know that?"

He just looked at me.

"My father's name was Mick too, but I knew Mickey Quinn. He was a good man. One of the best second-story men I ever met. Any son of Mickey Quinn automatically deserves my respect."

"What are you talking about? My dad worked down in the yards. He was as honest as the day was long. After I tried to be nice, why are you trying to piss me off Mr. Beech?"

"Don't take my word for it. There's others you could ask, Joe Battaglia for one. Mickey Quinn could open any door, any skylight or any transom. He had a gift for it."

"That's not true! What possible value is there in you trashing my father."

"I'm not trashing him. Mickey Quinn was an artist." He leaned back remembering and talked to the ceiling. "He was small, almost little. He was also an excellent 'wheel man'; he could drive anything and drive it well." He raised his hand in a gesture to show small height. "He could get into the smallest places. He was an incredible asset. Mickey Quinn deserved my friendship. At times, he was also my associate. It's a small world Agent Quinn."

"What! That can't be true, you're lying." I had moved from surprised to mad now. "Stop trying to get my goat Harry. You're pissing me off."

"Have you seen Sally lately? You should ask her. She knew Mickey too."

"Believe me I will, but Joe Battaglia told me to stay away from Sally."

Any lightness in Harry's expression melted faster than the popsicle in his hand.

"What did he say?" There was a hard edge in his raspy whisper.

"Stay away from Sally Square."

Harry sat quietly for a full minute, looking out into the hallway beyond the glass, chewing on the popsicle stick. Then he drew a long breath and blew it out through his teeth. He looked directly at me.

"Go see Sally. I'm asking you as a favor, as soon as you can, go see her and tell her this. Tell her Battaglia is watching her. Do this for me, Thomas please. It is important."

"Why?"

"Dominoes are starting to fall. Billy Duggar, Bobby Dey-Dey. Joe Battaglia's visit was a warning. One you should take seriously, but not before you go see Sally again."

I was shook by his big reveal. How could this possibly be true, and how did my father keep it a secret from us all those years if it was true? I needed to wrap my head around it, and I needed to study up on it.

"By this time he knows your Mickey Quinn's boy; he smells a rat. You need to watch your ass too."

"This is just some bullshit story."

Harry dropped his head back onto the pillow and looked out under his eyebrows.

"What was your father's middle name?"

"Francis."

He lowered his brows and winked. "Not many people knew Mickey Quinn."

Dad? Is that you?

My desk chair rolled all the way back to the wall behind me and I took a deep breath. Unbelievable! No way it could be true, except there it was. Laying open on my desk was an archives file I had pulled from the stacks. The file was ancient and thin, but not that thin. It bore the marks of a file that had been handled frequently and arrived on my desk quickly when I requested it.

I noted the name and was a little setback that the file even existed. The name on the file was Michael Francis. When I had flipped back the cover, the first thing that met my gaze was the mugshot on the left side of the folder, where my father gazed back up from the top of my desk.

There were very few photographs of my father ever taken. He was the one who usually ran the camera. Taking any pictures of family gatherings, making sure to include everyone, but never in front of the camera himself. I did not need them: pictures of my father. My father, for his small stature, occupied a huge position in my life. He was not just a breadwinner or my Daddy, he was a hero—he had been my hero. I had watched him walk into a room like he owned it. I watched as his brothers and sisters looked up to him. He had been a hero with quiet strength and a steady hand.

But there in black and white, my father gazed up at me. In front of the camera for a change. No smile, no saying 'cheese' for the picture, just name and arrest record number on a very serious face. The right side of the file detailed multiple incidents, 'unlawful entry, possession of stolen goods, trespassing, evading arrest, burglary, and grand theft. The last was a 1967 Pontiac GTO which oddly enough was found the next day still in mint condition and in the exact parking spot where it had been before it went missing. Apparently, the steering wheel and door handle had not been wiped completely clean, and when dusted, fingerprints were revealed that were previously accredited to one Michael Francis.

Incredibly, he had never been convicted. It seemed he had a guardian angel. He had come to the very edge a number of times, but never fallen into the crevasse. In an extended phone call with the Clerk of Courts, I had them pull several of the old files and read the results to me. Insufficient evidence, witnesses refusing to testify, witnesses not appearing and victims unsure of facts. Mickey Francis had been a very slippery fish when he hadn't been busy being Michael Quinn.

Sitting there in the dark of my office I reflected on my

childhood with a different perspective. I recalled the number of nights when my father would call and tell my mother he was working a 'double' or when he would be too tired to get out of bed in the morning after a long 'shift.' With a different set of eyes, I thought back to times when he would spend like a drunken sailor, treating us to extra candy or a ride on the Tilt-A-Whirl, taking us to Blackhawks hockey games and other times when we ate oatmeal days on end and soup was lunch and dinner. This time I recognized a different pattern. My training kicked in and I recognized my father but from a different point on the compass.

I looked back on my embattled mother. I remember when she would place her hands and forehead on the kitchen sink and bent at the waist, sob while my brothers and sisters romped around her. I remember her delighted laughs when my father would tease her with a jig around the kitchen and then pat her on the butt. How had she kept the secret, I wondered. I thought about my siblings. How many had had any inclination? My world shifted on a different axis and tilted into a whole new orbit.

How this little tidbit of information had slipped past the FBI I could not imagine. I had gone through extensive vetting; they had interviewed my friends, but there had not been any family to question. They were all gone by the time the FBI had become interested. They'd gone back over my school years and even uncovered a few of my teenage hijinks. Nowhere in their intensive search had they happened upon my criminal father or found even the slightest blemish on his record. It did not reinforce my faith in the bureau.

My second thought was whether I should bring the

matter up to anyone. Undoubtedly, it would probably mean the end of my law enforcement career if I did. I didn't imagine the bureau or my SAC would take too kindly to my keeping such a secret from them. This was such a blatant subversion of facts that it would appear to them that it had been deliberate. I would be out on the street and out of a job within minutes. And I liked my job —so far.

I rolled forward and powered up my computer. When it was ready, I accessed the FBI site and asked for an address and any and all information on my new person of interest. I asked for directions to Mr. Joseph Battaglia.

Burglar

I was so used to the rigamarole that the gate guard would put me through that I was surprised when he just basically waved me through. I had expected to be detained like in past experiences. Now I was going to arrive at Sally's earlier than I had planned.

To make things even stranger, there was no neighbor from across the street standing out in his yard when I drove up and no Sally greeting me from the front porch. The change in protocol made me a little nervous and I got up on my toes as soon as I stepped out of the car. It felt awkward to climb the front steps by myself and to find and ring the doorbell.

It had been a week since Joseph Battaglia had come into my apartment and my life. During that week, I'd learned a lot about him, where he lived, what he did or didn't do for a living and who many of his known associates were. Battaglia had an FBI file that was not thin in any respect. He had been arrested for a variety of transgressions and convicted on a few. Most had been of a local nature. There was nothing there to interest the FBI anymore, but there once had been. He had done time both at Marion State on a racketeering conviction and at Ossining in New York for jury tampering, but nothing in his record was more current than twenty years ago. Since getting released the last time, Mr. Battaglia appeared to have cleaned up his act. Or he had at least gotten smarter in his dealings.

Battaglia lived on the seventeenth floor on the north side of Chicago, along what people called the Gold Coast. High-rise, high-priced condos lining the lakefront with a view of the Michigan cities on the other side of the lake. He appeared to be retired with no visible means of income. He did not own a driver's license or have a voter's registration I.D. His immediate family history appeared to have been tragic. He had been married, his wife had died fourteen years ago from an unlisted cause and there had been an adopted son, also deceased.

In my heightened state of sensitivity, it was easy for me to imagine that he must still be connected to the wrong side of the law. And even easier for me to believe he would have connections to Harry Beech. But Harry's reaction to hearing his name had been instantly negative, so whatever connection they may have enjoyed it wasn't pleasant anymore, if it ever had been.

I had not exactly promised Harry that I would talk to Sally about Battaglia, but I hadn't discouraged it either. In truth, I appreciated the opportunity to see her again. Although, she was not a focus of my investigation, she did have some bearing on it. She was also just fun. She said what she thought and meant what she said. She was completely at ease with herself and totally in command of her world. She radiated gravitas and I learned something important every time I spent time with her.

I took one more glance at the empty front yard across the street and rang the doorbell.

"It's open. Please come in."

Stranger and stranger I thought and as I turned the knob and pushed open the door.

Anything I had anticipated when the door swung open went immediately out the window. The foyer was completely wrecked. The remains of a broken vase and its contents were splashed across the floor, and the small table it had stood on lay on its side, its legs broken. The tasteful runner was pushed aside in a rumpled heap against the foot of the staircase and standing in the center of the small room with his arms folded on his chest and a scowl on his face was the tough looking neighbor from across the street.

"In here Tom."

Her voice came from the sitting room to the left. The neighbor raised an eyebrow and tipped his head in the same direction. Without turning my back on him, I sidled around the corner and looked into the room.

Sally Carlisle sat quietly on the loveseat at the back of the room with a baseball bat resting across her knees. Another man sat alertly on the piano bench to her left. On the floor between them knelt another man with his hands clasped behind his back. The kneeling man was bent at the waist and his head hung down, blood dripping from his mouth and nose. I recoiled a step back and made contact with the neighbor coming into the room behind me.

"Easy Tom. It's not what you think. Well, maybe it is but not exactly what you think at least." Sally didn't move, but she raised one hand. "Let me explain."

"What the hell!"

"I know what it looks like but give me a second please."

"Have the police been called? What happened to him." I bent over and tried to look at the man's face. He turned and looked up through shaggy hair at me. "Buddy, are you alright? Sally what?"

Reflexively, my hand had risen to my holster but before I could think to use it another hand came down on top of mine.

"Easy big fella. Give her a minute."

I removed my hand and cocked my head to the side instead. "Well?"

"The guy behind you is Greg. This is Jerry over here. They're part of the 'uh' Neighborhood Watch around here. You've seen them before. I called them after I found this dirty fellow rifling around in my stuff." She toed the man on the floor with her shoe. "Weren't you?"

"He broke into your house?"

"He was here when I came back from running errands. Yes."

"So, you should have called the police, not beat the hell out of him. Now he can press charges Sally."

"He could maybe, but he won't." Her voice was calm and steady, "I needed to know what he was here for.

Which I still don't know." She hefted the bat in his direction.

"Sally! This is nuts. Normal people call the police. You should call the police immediately." I tried appealing to Jerry, sitting on the piano bench and got a non-committal shrug. "I can take him into custody, but this is a local jurisdiction. Sally, you need to call the police."

"We actually are going to have to. We gotta get this guy on ice for a while."

"I don't…what?"

"A couple hours in the ER and then into police custody. An hour after this guy hits the precinct station, he's gonna lawyer up. Once that happens, we're shit out of luck and I want to know why he picked my house."

"It's up to the police to investigate Sally."

"The police have a simple burglary suspect here. They get a few of them every day. This dope will plead it out, post bail and be back in business in no time."

"He needs to go to the hospital Sally."

"That'll buy us a few hours anyway. His pockets were empty, a set of car keys, but no wallet. He's not parked outside, so he got here on foot. That means he's parked nearby or he was dropped off. The gate guard hasn't let anyone in or out that wasn't expected, so he had to walk here from a different neighborhood."

"Sally, it's up to the police."

"The police will do their routine diligence; I want to just make sure that is all it is."

"Call the police."

"In a minute Tom. Jerry and Greg, you guys go around the neighborhoods and see if there's any cars parked nearby that don't look like they have a home. I'm going to call the police and Agent Quinn will be my witness when they get here. Use this dipshit's keys to try door locks on any car you find. If you find it, bring it back here so we can go through it. Quickly now, once the police are involved, the clock starts ticking."

Sally was in full command.

"Sally that's withholding evidence. I can't agree to something like that."

"We'll give the cops the keys once we're done with them Tom. 'They must have fallen out of his pocket when he fell out in the foyer. We didn't notice them right away because of the mess.' We'll be happy to return them as soon as we found them."

Jerry flipped the set of keys to Greg, and they both went out the front door.

"Keep an eye on him for me Tom. I left my phone in my purse out in the garage. I'll have to go get it to call."

||||||||||||||||||||||||||||||||||||

Once the call was made, the two-man police team arrived in a very short time. There was plenty of crime in a gated community but it usually involved infidelity, adultery or tax evasion and embezzlement. The hard-knuckled fun stuff crime rarely occurred for the local police force to be involved and demanded immediate, quick response. They were dutifully impressed when it became clear that this color-coordinated and stylish woman of a certain age had single handedly neutralized a burglar using a baseball bat and then had calmly reported it to the police.

The perp was dutifully handcuffed and then loaded in

an ambulance with one of the two police officers. The second one sat down on the loveseat and took our statements. Mine was easy. I was here on a separate matter to follow up on a different investigation and arrived after the incident had occurred. I had been expected and only arrived shortly before the call to the police. I had nothing to add or subtract from the situation, although I had utilized my own handcuffs and I was going to need them back.

Then came Sally's statement, and it was a wonder.

"Yes officer. I was expecting company so I went out to pick up a few things. When I arrived back home, I entered the kitchen from the garage, where I discovered that my back door was slightly ajar and the room was colder than it should have been. It worried me because I never forget to lock the house whenever I leave." She paused for dramatic effect, clutching her hands to her chest before continuing, "I keep a baseball bat near the door to chase away stray cats that try and catch the birds in my feeders. They are so pesky those cats. I've complained to the neighbors and neighborhood watch, but no one claims responsibility for those cats. Honestly officer, I almost wish someone would just shoot them. I do love seeing those birds, especially during the winter." She pointed out through the kitchen windows. "I keep the feeders full because I enjoy them so much."

She stopped like she'd lost her train of thought, "Oh the bat!…so I picked it up. I was coming down the hallway when this wretched person came out of my sitting room, right here in this doorway. I'm sorry, I just hit him with the bat. It must have been a reflex or something. I've never done anything like that before. I guess I just reacted by instinct."

"So you did this to him all by yourself, Mrs. Carlisle?"

"Yes, I guess I did. It's a little confusing. I was terrified and angry. Yes, angry. I might have hit him more than once—I think."

"Yes ma'am, it would seem so. We're going to need to take that baseball bat into custody for a while Mrs. Carlisle. I'm sure you understand."

"Oh? Really?" She looked reluctantly at the nasty thing. "Of course. I understand. Will I be able to get it back?"

"Once we get everything sorted out, of course ma'am. So nothing you know of that was taken?"

"Nothing that I can tell so far. It's all so confusing. I'll have to look around. If I find something was taken can I let you boys know?"

"Yes ma'am, certainly. Just call the station house and report it. I'm sure there will be a detective that will want to talk with you at some point soon. You could let him know too."

"That's good. Make sure to tell him to call ahead though please. I'll be a little nervous now about strangers." Then she put her hand on his shoulder and simpered, "You guys do such excellent work. Thank you. Please remember to call me when it's time for your next fundraiser. You have my number."

It was the side of Sally that you would never expect to see, but then when you did see it, it answered a whole lot of other questions that you didn't know you had until that moment.

I Know

Sally sat at the end of the kitchen counter. She had just refilled a champagne flute in her hand, it wasn't her first and they were going down fast. The sounds of an impact wrench came dimly through from the garage. Greg and Jerry were busy taking apart the car that the recovered keys had fit. From the sound of it, they were being very diligent.

"If there's anything to find, the boys will find it pretty quick."

"Sally, I've got a few issues with this."

"Oh relax Tom. You aren't on duty are you?"

"I'm an FBI agent Sally, technically I'm always on duty. Besides, I walked right into the middle of this and this just isn't right."

"Tom. I found an intruder in my home. Almost accidentally I neutralized the individual and then I called the police. He was remanded into custody and I filed a statement." She waved her flute. "What else could I possibly be required to do?"

"C'mon Sally. There are two heavy-set guys out in your garage taking someone else's car apart. They're searching for God knows what and I'm sitting in your kitchen watching you drink champagne. I can't relax into something like that."

Sally put her glass down, crossed her arms, set her elbows on the counter and fixed him with a hard look. I suddenly saw the resemblance to her brother.

"Like it or not Tom you are a part of what is happening here. I didn't plan or choreograph this but here we are. Whether the boys find anything or not, tomorrow we'll turn the keys over to the police and that will be the end of it as far as legal law enforcement is concerned."

She rose from her stool, walked down the counter toward me, and leaned down to make eye contact.

"That guy was here for a reason Tom and it wasn't burglary." She raised her right hand and dropped a six-inch stiletto knife on the counter. "He wasn't here to rob or steal Agent Tom Quinn; he was here for me."

I looked down at the knife. It was a beautiful thing, crystal clear with a sparkling handle. Formed out of a clear acrylic or some other heavy polymer. It would pass through any metal detector on the planet. I looked up and met her intense gaze. "I know."

"What do you mean?" She recoiled, "You know?"

"If I'm not mistaken, Joseph Battaglia sends his regards."

"Shit and son of a bitch!"

"Harry sent me to tell you to watch your ass. That's why I called you."

"Harry's a little late."

"He told me last week; I thought it could wait. I apologize."

"You thought it could wait? Seriously?"

"Well, he was pretty low key about it. He said to get in touch with you when I could."

"That's when you should take it most seriously. Honestly Tom! You gotta' start paying more attention."

"Well I'm here now, aren't I."

"A day late and a dollar short."

"Sorry. Battaglia came to my apartment and warned me. He told me to stay away from you."

"What! Seriously? Old Joe said that? He's getting a little big for his britches if he thinks he's got anything to say about what I do."

"Well I think he just demonstrated how long his reach might be, Sally."

"Son of a bitch! You think?"

Mickey Quinn

She got up and walked to the door to the garage. Opening she yelled, "Boys!"

When the sound of the wrench stopped,

"C'mon in here for a few minutes."

In a matter of minutes, we were seated around the kitchen counter. Beer for the two men, whiskey for me and champagne for Sally.

"Okay, what did you find Greg?"

"Nothin' SQ. It's a rental. The receipt and the papers are in the glove box."

"Okay, put it back where you found it. Drop a dime bag in the console."

"Excuse me!"

"Relax Tom. You're an observer. You'll get your

chance."

"He's already in the hospital and then the jail. It'll be a while before he appears before the magistrate."

"It'll be a little longer now."

"Sally that's a criminal act."

It was either Greg or Jerry that pushed back from the counter and stood up. I couldn't tell them apart. I hadn't actually thought that I was going to need to.

"You gotta' problem fed?"

"I'm saying that what you are doing is illegal. Technically, I'm supposed to report it or arrest you even. It's my job." I stood up and faced him. "I like my job."

I stood there staring him down, but he didn't flinch. Finally, he sighed and shrugged and sat.

"Boy's settle down please. Greg at ease, please. Let's just relax."

I shrugged back at Greg, sat down and leaned over my drink, but fixed my eyes on her.

"That's better. Now, first of all, Tom. These two handsome fellows are my nephews, not just my neighbors. They're my brother Andy's boys. I trust them completely. They moved into the neighborhood shortly after Andy died. We keep an eye out for each other. Battaglia knows that, so he's pushing his luck if he thinks he can pull something like this. He must have believed his warning would be enough for you Tom."

"They came to my place on Tuesday night."

"They? Who's they?" It was Jerry who asked.

"Battaglia and two goons with him. They were there when I got home from work. They let themselves into my place." I paused for dramatic effect but none of them seemed phased in the least. "He told me to leave Harry alone, just drop it. Then he told me that he knew I was visiting you too and he told me to leave you alone. I actually thought he was looking out for your welfare, but Harry took it pretty seriously.”

“Harry takes everything seriously. You never knew when it was going to matter back in the day.” She smiled, nodded to the two men and then frowned at me. “Well then, what took you so long?”

“I work for a living Sally. I waited until I could get away from work. It’s only Saturday Sally, I didn’t think it was life or death. Turns out I was wrong; looks like.”

“You think?”

“I don’t like you sharing all this with a feebee SQ. Why is he still here anyway?”

“Well for one thing, he’s the only way we have of communicating with Harry. That’s reason enough, but he’s also witnessed a lot of this, so maybe if we’re nice to him, he’ll look the other way a little.”

She got up, took two more beers from the refrigerator and distributed them. Then she poured another glass of champagne. Picking up the whiskey bottle, she held it up to the light and addressed it, “And maybe he’s just a little bit more.”

“What do you mean by that?” I was honestly offended by her inference.

She walked down the counter and poured a healthy amount into my glass, “Boys, he’s an FBI agent for sure and might be a good one someday, but he’s also something else to us. Boys, this is Mickey Francis’ boy.”

I was surprised but not as much as the other two.

“No shit? No fuckin’ shit?”

“Sally? How did…when did you know that?”

"Mr. Quinn," she smiled and touched the forelock of hair I had hanging down onto my forehead. "You have his eyes, his hair and you speak with his voice. You're taller and wider than he was, but if I heard you speak and couldn't see you, I'd think it was Mickey himself back from the grave. I knew it the day you walked up the driveway and called me ma'am. Mickey Francis was my dear friend. I miss him and his sense of humor almost every day."

I looked the question up at her, and she nodded. "Yes, and that way too."

"Shit."

"Put's you in a 'rock and a hard place' situation, doesn't it Tom?"

"You got that right."

"Wait. What d'ya mean?" Greg was trying to catch up.

"Tom here got into the FBI under false pretenses you see. If they'd found out he was related to Mickey Francis they would have never allowed him to join the bureau. Isn't that true Tom?"

"Yes. If they found out tomorrow, I'd probably be out. It seems to be true and I'm stuck in the middle."

"Nonsense Tom. There's the right and the wrong. Just because it's illegal doesn't mean it's wrong, and just because someone else is in charge doesn't mean they're right."

"I know it's not black and white, but it's not up to you to decide right and wrong either."

"We each have to decide individually what's right and wrong. If I asked you to shoot Greg, you'd say that was wrong and you wouldn't do it. Right?"

"Of course."

"But if Greg was threatening to kill me with a knife, you'd shoot him to protect me."

"Possibly."

"You'd make an instantaneous decision. Right or wrong. You would act?"

"Hopefully."

"Don't be so hard on yourself. Of course you would. Well our right and wrong takes a little longer than instantaneously, but that doesn't make it wrong either."

"What's your point?"

"Your secret is safe with us Tom—for now. We are going to need some answers and we are going to need to do a few things that will be right for us. You can choose to help, or you can step back, but now we have your secret Tom. You must not let your secret become a favor that you owe to someone who holds your secret. If we're going to the mats, and we're not sure who all the bad guys are yet Tom, we're going to need you to watch our backs. We want you on our team Tom."

A Favor

It was Sunday, so I got to meet a few guards who were different from the ones I usually did when I ran the usual guard gauntlet. But in jail, every day is pretty much the same as any other day unless you punch a time clock, so they weren't really that interested in me. I was such a regular visitor that up until now I'd only been greeted with raised eyebrows and shoulder shrugs, but no real interest. I made my way through the warren of corridors and elevators until once again I was looking through the glass at Harry Beech. He watched me standing there, and for the first time he nodded, but only just a little.

The orderly let me into the suite, and Harry raised his bed to a sitting position.

"It's Sunday."

"Yes."

"Did you go to church this morning Mr. Quinn?"

"I don't go to church anymore Harry."

"What would your momma say?"

"She would say a rosary and take communion."

"So, this is how you spend your Sunday afternoons? Not taking a leisurely drive or the corner tap to watch a football game. Working?"

"I'm not here for work." I hadn't moved to my usual seat, instead I stood at the foot of his bed and gave him my most serious look.

He got the message and you could see that he immediately clocked in.

"Something has happened."

"Watch for the orderly."

I stepped into the corner of the room, away from the glass. I put my foot up on the stupid chair that I hated and pulled up my pants leg. Pulling the tape loose and with as little hair removal as possible, I pulled the stiletto knife off my inner calf where I had taped it. Turning, I dropped the knife onto the bedcovers.

Harry looked down at it. Then he looked out through the glass for a long minute.

"Are you expecting me to put my fingerprints on this or something?"

"No."

"You're not here to use it on me. It's too late for that."

"No."

"It's a nice piece, yours?"

"No."

"Well what?"

"It was a message."

Harry looked at the little dagger and then out the glass as the orderly passed. Then he turned and met my eyes.

"Sally?"

"Yes."

"She okay?"

"Yes."

"Who?"

"Big money's on Battaglia."

"You gone off the reservation Agent Quinn?"

"Not entirely and not yet."

I picked up the stiletto and dropped it into my coat pocket. They don't search you going out, only in. I knocked on the glass for the orderly.

"See you tomorrow Harry."

Nope

"Nope."

"I just need a little time off. I didn't think it would but that visit from Joe Battaglia really kinda' upset me."

"Tom. You're a combat veteran. Twice decorated for bravery. Wounded in battle multiple times. You've cleared all the psych hurdles. I wouldn't give you the time off even if I could. You don't have any time in grade Tom. You just haven't been here long enough to have earned any time, and this just doesn't sound like some psycho killing event." He leaned across the desk. "Unless there's something else?"

"No, I'm just having trouble sorting it out."

"Well sort it out in your spare time, or come clean. That's always an option."

I looked at him, then the wall behind him, then down at my shoes. "Okay."

"Okay, what?"

It took about three minutes to give him the details of the breaking and entering at Sally Carlisle's. I left the part out about the stiletto.

"So what?

"So, I think something's going on."

"You're detailed to sit with Harry Beech. If he tells you anything. Anything at all. You write it down. You report it. That's your job Quinn. It doesn't say anything about going out on tangents and expanding investigations where they're not warranted."

"I think there's more here than a simple B&E."

"How so?"

"I think it's got something to do with Harry Beech."

"Like what?

"I don't know yet."

"You got any solid evidence?"

"No".

"Then no."

"C'mon chief. The burgler was arraigned by Zoom or something from his hospital bed yesterday while he was still in the hospital. I can't get any other info on the dude.

They don't share. The locals don't want him in the system though, so he'll make bail by this afternoon. I just want to ask him a few questions. Can't we do that at least?"

"What kind of questions are you going to ask him, if you don't know how he's involved?"

"I'll think of some."

"You're taking this Sally Carlisle thing too far Tom.

The answer's no. Let it go."

"That's what a lot of people are saying to me these days. 'Let it go.' I'm just trying to get you some results, but I don't know exactly where to look."

"Jeezus. Fine. But don't start thinking that favors grow on trees. I'll make a few calls. Check back with me in a couple hours."

The Jeweler

The parked cars on both sides of the street narrowed the street down to one lane. Street lights on the corners and middle of the block illuminated the silhouettes of rats as they crossed back and forth in the half-light. The tavern on the corner had just turned off its window lights and soon the interior lights winked out one at a time. Before the last one went off, the front door swung open and a figure reeled out and down the front steps.

He recovered on the sidewalk and then paused. Fishing in his pockets, he pulled out a cigarette and lit it with a lighter from his other pocket. Once he had it going, he struck off down the sidewalk with no hint in his gait that he had spent the night in a corner bar. As he made his way down into the darker part of the block, I opened my car door and stepped out onto the sidewalk to block his way. He stopped and looked me up from my heels to my hat.

"The fuck you want?"

From the other side of the car Greg and Jerry got out and walked around behind him.

"Son of a bitch, honest, I don't know nothin.'"

Greg stepped up behind him and put a hand on his shoulder.

"Shit!"

"Would you mind stepping over to the vehicle then sir?"

"What if I don't?"

"Then these two gentlemen will assist you."

He stepped across to the car and I opened the rear passenger door.

"Get in please."

I took the seat across from him and Greg and Jerry got in the front.

"It's too cold to stand outside and have a chat. This is a little warmer and more comfortable."

"Speak for yourself jagoff."

"Honestly Mr. Arnold. I just have one question I want to ask you. If you don't mind. It's no big deal and I promise nothing,...nothing will come out of your answer one way or the other—as long as your answer is an honest one."

"How you gonna' know if my answer is honest?"

"Because we already know the answer."

"Then why you gotta ask in the first place?"

"Because your answer might foster a few more questions. That is if you don't mind. You're the Jeweler after all. Right?"

"Mind? Why would I mind? I'm just minding my own goddammed business walking home and I get abducted. It's two o'fuckin'clock in the morning but they have questions. So the world stops because they have questions. Do I mind answering a few questions instead of going home to bed, and maybe getting a piece of ass before I fall asleep? No. No please, ask me all the fuckin' questions that you want. I'm not busy."

"It's just a simple question, really sir. One answer, and you're on your way. Promise."

"Let's get it over with. What? What could possibly not wait until the light of day to ask me?"

"Aren't you who they call the Jeweler?"

"So what?"

"Do you recognize this?"

I unrolled the towel that I'd wrapped the beautiful stiletto in between us on the seat. The interior light danced off the jeweled handle and glinted off the razor-sharp edges.

"Where did you get this?" All trace of stubbornness had disappeared instantly, instead his voice was incredulous.

"Would you be surprised if I told you I found it *in* someone?"

He looked up quickly, shocked and questioning.

"A friend dropped it." I smiled back at him. "It's beautiful, isn't it."

"Yes, yes," he stroked a finger down the handle. "Yes she is. Yes, I loved this piece. These are real gemstones in the handle, rubies and garnets, see?" He turned it in the light so that it sparkled. "The balance between blade and handle is perfect. It will never dull, well almost never, and the ceramic composite will never set off a metal detector. It's almost perfect."

Look for 'The Jeweler.' That's what Harry had told me on Sunday before I left his room. There are other craftsmen, but this piece is special. The Jeweler will be the one. He'll know.

He hadn't been hard to find. Stanley Arnold had been a skilled jeweler in his own right. He had gained a reputation in authentic reproductions. He could duplicate any piece of jewelry almost perfectly, but for far less money. He had become the darling of insurance fraud and had never lacked for work. But along the way, something had slipped. Suddenly, and for no apparent reason, a little over a decade ago, he had stopped working, stopped creating, and crawled into a bottle. Apparently, everyone had watched him disintegrate into that bottle of whiskey. They all knew of his demise and everyone knew where to find him. They had all watched in despair at the destruction of an artist destroyed from the inside out.

"Who bought it from you?"

"Bought it? No this is too beautiful; I could never have sold it." He touched it with a fingertip. "It is the best I've ever made."

"Then why don't you still have it?"

"It was a gift. I gave it as a gift."

"Bullshit."

"No really, I gave it to her." He started to get emotional and he choked a little. "I thought it would be a fitting ornament, something deadly but beautiful. Like her."

"Who is her exactly?"

"You guys don't know nothin.'"

"That's right. We don't know nothin', so fill us in."

"What if I tell you I don't feel like it?"

"Then I think Jerry would like to get to know you a little better."

"Shit- easy. You smell like a cop."

"You hear that Jerry? He says you smell like a cop."

"I said you do."

"C'mon, we're all friends here. We're just tying up a loose end Mr. Arnold. Just play along for a minute or two. Please?"

"Okay, okay…I gave it to her."

"Who's her?"

"To Miranda. I gave it to Miranda."

"Who, pray tell is Miranda?"

"Who was she, you mean."

"Okay, who was Miranda?"

"You know. Miranda Dugan."

"How do I know that name?"

"She was the best." He sniffed and ran his coat sleeve across his eyes. "Right up until Harry Beech killed her. Shot her like a dog in the street."

Research

I rolled back in my chair, still staring at the computer screen. It was there; I'd just missed it. Originally I'd done my homework superficially on Harry. I'd glossed the file and called it done. Now, six weeks later, I suddenly needed to do my homework all over again. Only this time I really needed to study it. I'd just assumed it was a few anonymous victims that I didn't need to know about or had no relevance.

> Miranda Dugan, thirty-four year old female, deceased. Cause of death, multiple gunshot wounds. She had been shot four times in all, two struck her in the back, a third in the left armpit and as she turned the fourth at the base of her throat at close

range, apparently as she ran from her assailant. It was either that or she had opened her front door for her assailant and then turned her back on them because she knew them. The murder weapon had been a .38 caliber revolver recovered at the scene. Blood spatter supported that all four shots had hit her as she fled. Three rounds had passed through her entirely, probably due to her proximity to the shooter. The back of her blouse showed powder burns emphasizing the extremely short range from which the shots had been fired. The exit wounds had resulted in subsequent gunshot wounds secondarily to a dependent male infant child.

Jonathan Dugan, 6 month-old male, in her arms at time of assault also resulting in fatality.

23 month-old female Samantha Dugan deceased, cause of death, water aspiration —she had drowned in the kitchen sink.

Thomas Janes, 43 year-old male deceased. Cause of death gunshot wound to the frontal aspect of skull.

I studied the crime scene. Blood spatter patterns supported all gunshots had originated in or near the front doorway. Entry wounds in Miranda supported a weapon held at approximately shoulder height and fired at a 10-14 degree downward angle. Janes was found lying on his back with his feet on the front porch and his upper body extending through the doorway and into the small foyer.

> Harry Beech age 58, apprehended at the scene less than three feet away from the deceased Janes. Apparent murder weapon showed his fingerprints on the grip and barrel.

In fact, Janes had been found lying on his back halfway in and halfway out of the front door. Ms. Dugan had been found within ten feet of the front door. In her last dying effort she had turned her body to avoid falling on her infant child. It had made no difference in the end.

Apparently, prior to his death, Mr. Janes had tracked through the blood spatter enough to get some on the soles of his shoes before dying in the front doorway. Shoeprints had been detected in other parts of the house, especially the kitchen. Both men wore the same size shoes. Beech had tested positive for gunpowder residue on his right hand. Harry had been taken into custody at the scene and refused any statement. He had made only one statement during his arraignment or his trial. He'd only said it once and never again.

"There is no justice."

Reflection

There was a physician in his room when I arrived. Harry sat up with his gown pulled down while the doctor listened to his chest. I had the orderly let me in and I tried to be quiet during the examination. Harry made eye contact with me as I arranged myself on the uncomfortable chair in the corner. The doctor ignored me. After the examination, the doctor wrapped his stethoscope around his neck, nodded at me before he left, but before he could separate entirely, I caught up with him in the hallway.

"So doctor?"

"Are you family?"

"Sort of."

"What does sort of mean?"

"FBI."

"Then it's none of your business."

"I'm trying not to impinge on him too much. He has no family that can see him here, so I'm trying to connect between his immediate family and Harry. It's the only way that they can do it. Harry and I have a sort of arrangement."

"What sort of arrangement would that be?"

"He talks to me when he feels like it and verbally abuses me during the other times."

"So, he likes you."

"I wouldn't say that."

"Me either." He half smiled and turned to go.

"Can you tell me anything?"

"Sure." He shrugged into his coat. "He doesn't have much longer."

"How much longer is 'not much longer'?"

"I guess we'll see."

"Not good enough Doc. C'mon I kinda need to know. Just the fact that I'm here and he's okay with that should mean something."

"Okay. Look his lungs are starting to fill up. His heart is working hard to compensate but pneumonia is right around the corner for him. When that happens, his kidneys will fail and he'll die." He sighed and looked at Harry through the glass. "He's already tougher than I thought he was, so I can't guess what the timetable might be."

"Two weeks, a month, maybe longer?"

"All of the above. Buckle up. We'll see what happens."

The One and Only

Tuesday morning, I was at the county lock-up bright and early. I wanted to see him as soon after breakfast as possible. Maybe catch him in a good mood. And maybe catch him before he might be taken for another hearing and disappear into the wind. When they brought him to the interview room, he looked surprised to see me. For my part, I didn't think Bradley Simonsen looked any better than the last time I saw him. Granted, he was wearing a clean orange jumpsuit instead of the filthy sweatshirt he'd had on then, and his nose wasn't bleeding any more. It even looked like he might have washed his hair. But the left side of his face was the color of a ripe eggplant and his left eye was swelled almost entirely shut.

It turned out that I had been in a panic for no reason.

After Bradley had been released from the local Emergency Department, Mr. Simonsen had been immediately placed under arrest. During his arraignment, bail had been denied. It had come as no surprise to anyone that he had a few prior involvements with the legal system, but at least one of them had resulted in an outstanding warrant for a bail-jumping violation. With no effort on my part, I now had all the time in the world to have a little chat with him. He wasn't going anywhere—for a while anyway.

The guard escort got him seated and left us alone. When he eased himself into the chair it appeared that there were other things that hurt than his face.

Bradley narrowed his good eye at me and fixated on the shield hanging in the breast pocket of my jacket. "Fuck."

"Can I get you a glass of water, maybe coffee?"

"I got nothin' to say to you."

"You can have a lawyer present if you want."

"Sure I can." He huffed. "That worthless piece of shit, he's already been and gone. Gave me a full ten minutes of his valuable time. From now on, I'll be part of his *busy schedule*."

"He wasn't too helpful?"

"He was fuckin' useless."

"That sucks."

"Like you could give two shits."

"Actually, you're right, I don't give two shits. So you see, we already agree on something."

"Fuck you."

"C'mon, how about we remember our manners? I'm trying to be polite. I have a couple questions and they're ones you might actually want to answer."

"What if I don't?"

"No sweat, you go your way, I'll go mine."

"That's all?"

"Well, there's the matter of a very sharp knife that may or may not have your fingerprints on it, also discovered at the crime scene and suddenly turning up as evidence. Something that might, maybe could, elevate the simple B&E to an armed robbery, minimally. But yeah, you and I, we'd be done with each other, no problem."

"I don't know anything about something like that. What are you trying to prove?"

"Nothing. The damned thing turned up after the police left. It's such a special thing and the lady of the house didn't recognize it, so I just hung on to it."

"So?"

"So," I leaned across the table, "it was yours. Wasn't it?"

Instead of an answer, he pushed back from the table and ran his hand through his long hair. Then he surprised me, leaned up to the table, and put both hands on the top, palms down.

"You're trying to leverage me. Tryin' to make me give something up, but I won't. I can't. It's mine alright? There's nobody…nothing else to give up. I don't have anyone or anything else left to give up. I ditched it when they nipped me. It's special, but it was mine."

"That's bullshit. The thing's worth a small fortune."

"I know. I coulda' got plenty for it if I wanted to, but I couldn't let it go. It's mine. It's all I've had left to show."

"Show?"

"Look, you go ahead and nail me with it if you want. I

don't care anymore. I took my shot, the bitch won. Fuck her, and fuck you too."

"C'mon Bradley, where'd you get something like that? You stole it, didn't you?"

"Fuck you." He almost whispered it.

"It's a beautiful thing Brad. It belongs in a museum or in a display case somewhere. What are you doing with it?"

"You wouldn't understand."

"Try me."

"It was hers okay! It's all I have left of her."

"Hers?"

"It was hers. It belonged to her, my sister, 'Randa."

"Randa?"

"Yeah, my sister Miranda Dugan."

"What happened to her?"

"I thought you didn't care."

"I don't care, but now I am interested."

"She was murdered. Killed by another guy who just did not give two shits either."

"Shit. Did they get the guy?"

"Yeah, they got him cold, the son-of-a-bitch."

"Did he go down for it?"

"Yeah, he got life, but that don't bring my sister back. So now I'm gonna take his sister away from him."

"You mean Sally Carlisle? Harry Beech is her brother, right? It was Harry Beech that killed your sister?"

"The one and only."

"Do you know why?"

"Why do you care?"

"I'm trying to trace the knife, but you brought this up. I'm just being polite."

"Yeah sure, I know why. She was desperate. She needed a job. She went back to Harry."

"Wait? She went *back* to Harry?"

"Yeah, she used to work for him. She was good too, you know?"

"Being good for Harry could have more than one meaning. Good how?"

"You know, odd jobs. A little here, a little there."

"So…?"

"That's all. When Harry had a job, you know, uh, that needed resolution. He'd call Randa sometimes."

"I don't understand."

"Are you stupid man? She was an escort; she was beautiful and she was really good. She got results, so she got plenty of work."

"So, what happened?"

"She fell in love. She wanted to get married, get clean you know. She didn't want to do the wet work anymore. She wanted to settle down and have babies. So she did, and she had two wonderful kids, but the marriage didn't make it. He was a small man and she was bigger than he was. He couldn't handle her reputation; he got smaller and she got bigger. When he left her, he left her with a mortgage and a shitload of bills she couldn't pay. So she went back to Harry, you know. But Harry said no; he told her she'd gotten clean and shouldn't try to get back in. She got desperate, hounding Harry to let her back in. When Harry'd had enough, he put a bullet in her and the kids to shut 'em up."

"Wet work? You said she was doing wet work for Harry?"

"All that kind of stuff went through Harry."

"But she was a woman; you said she was an escort. She was doing contract work? I don't get it. A woman?"
"All the best ones are women."

No Justice

Harry's eyes never left me when I entered the room. I took my time getting settled down in my chair. I crossed my legs and arms and looked across at him. I had deliberately procrastinated and not visited him for almost a week. My view of my situation, including Harry Beech and Sally Carlisle, had experienced a considerable upgrade. After the time I spent with Bradley Simonsen, I went back to the archives. There was something about the original crime that just wasn't right, and it made my brain itch as I tried to puzzle it out.

Miranda Simonsen-Dugan had multiple encounters with the police. Mostly detained and suspected of solicitation. She also had an uncanny talent for accumulating traffic tickets but not paying for them.

There was nothing else to support her brother's allegations. There was nothing in her file that even smelled of Harry Beech.

That was not the case with the other adult victim. Thomas Janes had a rap sheet that spanned three decades. He had been tried as an adult at seventeen for his part in a drive-by shooting but acquitted for lack of evidence. After that, he had been arrested multiple times for a variety of occupational endeavors. He had done time twice, once for possession and intent to distribute narcotics. The second time he'd gotten ten years and served eight for vehicular manslaughter. He had a long list of committed violent acts, usually on women, that the police would arrest him for, only to have charges dropped later on by the victims.

Tonight, Harry sat in his bed and stared at me. Even after so few days, he had sagged farther into the bed; like a candle left in the sun, he was slowly melting away. I knew he was burning to know if I had found anything out about the stiletto, but I had a different direction to go in now. I still had the itch, but I was starting to get a feel for where I wanted to go with it.

"How you feelin' Harry?"

"Like dog shit under a heat lamp."

"You look worse."

"Aren't you nice for noticing." He pushed himself up in the bed. "Where have you been? I was starting to think I was rid of you."

"I have been busy. Turns out there's a lot of catching up to do for guys like me."

"Like what?"

"Why don't you just ask me what it is you want to know Harry?"

"I don't want to know nothin', I'm dyin.' Remember?"

"I remember, but for now, you're still here."

"Damn right."

I didn't respond, but I switched my legs and crossed them the other way.

"So?" He asked.

"So?"

"So? What about the Jeweler?"

"What about him?"

"C'mon. You're just making this a lot harder than it needs to be. I'm just asking a simple question."

"I've got questions. That's never made any difference to you."

"There's good questions and bad questions. Some of them shouldn't be answered, and some of them should be obvious."

"How about we trade?"

"Forget it."

"No skin off my nose. You've been busting my balls for six weeks now. I can find out my own answers. But thanks for the tip on the Jeweler; it helped."

"You found him?"

"I didn't say that."

"Okay, okay…did you find the Jeweler?"

"That's better. Yes I did."

"Well?"

"First me."

"One question. I might not answer it though."

"What really happened to Mencorini?"

"Jeez!" He sank a little farther down on the bed again and took a couple of deep breaths through the nasal cannula. "C'mon?"

"I found the Jeweler. He knew the piece like you said. Actually, he made it himself. You could tell it was valuable to him. He had given it away to someone he cared about as a gift. He hadn't seen it since."

"Who'd he give it to?"

"Uh, uh, uh."

"Give me a break. Mencorini took a dirt nap. Okay? I didn't provide it, but there were a couple other people tired of his shenanigans. He died the same week he shot me."

"What happened to him?"

"Uh, uh, uh." He whispered.

"The Jeweler gave the stiletto to Miranda Dugan."

The revelation hit Harry like an open-palmed slap across the face. He recoiled and what little color he had evaporated instantly. He slumped down and his eyes rolled up in his head. His head started nodding back and forth, and he let out a small groan. Instantly, I was on my feet and pushed the orderly button hanging from the side of his bed.

Within seconds the orderly burst into the room. The gantry with all of Harry's instruments blinked, flashed, and demanded immediate attention with multiple alarms. The orderly stood at his bedside and watched the instruments but did not interfere.

"Aren't you going to do something?"

"Like what, he's got a DNR. I can't do anything, even if I wanted to. Which I do not."

The little robot in the corner wheezed in and out. Taking its time, unperturbed by the other instruments' panic. Harry's sunken chest rose and fell in unison with it.

His eyes looking up through his eyebrows, stared at nothing, his pupils blown wide open.

"What did you do to him?"

"Nothing. He asked me a question but he didn't like the answer I guess."

I started messing with the bed, moving levers, and not having much luck.

"What're you trying to do?"

"Lower his head and raise his leg. That's not trying to resuscitate him, is it?"

"No. But why?"

"Because we're playing twenty questions and it's my turn."

"I'll adjust the bed; just stop messing with it." He pushed me aside and flipped a couple levers. "Then I'm leaving. I have to report the incident in the log."

"Do what you gotta do. I'll be staying."

"Do what you gotta do."

I looked down at Harry. As his vitals slowly stabilized and the robot in the corner continued its monotonous wheeze. He still hadn't blinked.

"God dammit Harry. What the hell? What was she to you?"

I paced the small room a few laps. I'd asked myself the same question so many times it was a chant in the back of my mind. Harry's reaction was not one I would have expected from someone who had shot her four times at close range. It appeared emotional and seismically so. It had almost shut down his body on the spot.

On one of the laps, Harry finally blinked. After a little while longer, he moved his hand and then rolled his head in my direction. As recognition slowly dawned on him,

"Fuck." He wheezed out. "Still here."

"Gave me a bit of a scare there Harry. I still got my question though. I thought you were gonna make me wait."

"Fuck."

"C'mon Harry, I just got the one. It's an easy one."

"What?" He rasped, "What's the question?"

"Where did it go Harry? The sixth bullet? The gun was empty. Where'd the sixth bullet go Harry?"

It was the second time you could see the impact of the question. His eyes snapped up to meet my own. The look wasn't angry or confused. It was hopeful.

"You're a smart guy; you figure it out." He closed his eyes, took a deep breath, and sighed. "Now get lost."

Instincts

"Listen Tom. The FBI doesn't do a lot of its own investigating anymore. We fight crime with a laptop and computer screen. That usually means we spend a lot of time sitting at our desk monitoring activity. You've been missing a lot of that time Tom, so catch me up."

"It's not much."

"I insist. Give me what you've got."

"The kid that broke into the Carlisle house was just a penny-ante crook. Plenty of history back in the neighborhood but no big reputation. He has a lot of prior activities. He jumped his last bail so he's on ice; denied bail after he blew the last one."

"Okay." The Chief hadn't changed his posture; he was leaning forward, and the cigarette smoking in the ashtray was forgotten. "But that's got nothing to do with your current assignment. What about anything that you're supposed to be working on?"

"Okay. Well Jimmy Mencorini was killed the same week that he shot Harry Beech, but Beech swears he didn't do the deed. He said that it was someone else who had dealings with Jimmy, but I got the impression that the deal with the shooting hastened the inevitable."

"No idea who? Or where?"

"No. Not yet anyway."

"Anything else?"

"The woman that Harry killed, Miranda Dugan. Her maiden name was Simonsen. Ring any bells with you?"

"Nope, should it?"

"The kid that broke into Sally Carlisle's place, his last name was Simonsen too."

"You don't say?"

"I do say, and I think there's a connection."

"So far your instincts have been pretty good, but don't chase it too far. Stay with Harry for God's sakes."

"Just one more thing."

"Hmm?" He picked up his cigarette and leaned back."

"The gun at the crime scene."

"What about it?"

"It was a Ruger Six, all of the cylinders had been fired, but forensics only logged five of the six. There was one bullet unaccounted for."

"So?"

"So where did it go?"

"At this point, who cares?"

"I'm just grinding on it; I've got it stuck in my head. Like where did it go? All the shots fired were directed into the house. All but one.”

“Well don’t waste your time on it. It’s ancient history. Anything else?”

“How steady, numbers-wise, have gangland killings been over the last twenty years or so? Have they gone up or down since Harry went behind bars? He’s been in for almost ten years now, I’d like to know if the numbers changed. You know, like after he went in.”

“That’s a good idea. I’ll ask Cheryl to look it up; you can check with her. But give her a couple days to put it together.”

“Thanks for cutting me the slack Chief. I’m interested to see if there are any bumps and dips. Especially around the time of the Simonsen murders.”

“You mean Dugan.”

“Yeah, Dugan.”

Good Evening

There was a large black Lincoln Navigator idling in the driveway when I pulled up in front of the house. Seemingly overnight, the gate guard had taken to waving me through without the usual game of question and delay. Curious, I parked, walked past the great monstrosity, and met Sally coming out the front door. She ordinarily dressed like she had dinner plans, but this night she was dressed 'to the nines' as they say. She had a long dark-colored sheath dress that shimmered in the front porch lights, very high heels and she was wrapped in a full-length fur coat.

"You are just in time Tom. We're going for a ride. Climb on in, you can come along and we can talk."

"Where are you going? You look pretty fancy to be

just going for a ride Sally."

"I'm going to visit an old friend, but I'd like to hear any news you might have. Besides you're good company, so far anyway."

"I can just come back some other time."

"Nonsense, we're all going. It'd be a shame if we didn't take you too."

"That sounds ominous. Who's the friend?"

"Why none other than Mr. Joseph Battaglia himself. You won't want to miss it. I promise."

The drive downtown was brief to the high-rent district north of Oak Street. Sally rode in back with me. The two neighbors, Greg and Jerry, rode up front. In place of their usual too-tight polo shirts, they were both dressed in suits. True to form though, the jackets looked tight across the chest and shoulders.

When we pulled up to the address, Sally was the first one out on the sidewalk where she kept her back turned while the boys negotiated with the valet to park on the street and not in the parking garage underneath the building. I was starting to get increasingly uncomfortable. Battaglia had been clear in his message to stay away and even though he wouldn't do anything to me tonight, he had demonstrated that he already knew where I lived.

Once the parking negotiations were completed, we pushed through the entrance doors into a spotless lobby brightly lit with faux gold sconce lighting, carved plaster ceilings and terrazzo floor tile. From behind an ornate front desk the security guard only had eyes for Sally as the rest of us hung back. Sally's heels clicked on the floor as she strode forward all business.

"We're here to see Dorothea Federovski in 1748.

Would you please call the elevator for us?"

The mirrored elevator required a security key to call for a floor. Which the guard was more than happy to do for Sally but maybe not so much for the rest of us. Once it arrived we all piled in. It was not particularly spacious once Jerry and Greg stepped in. I found myself wishing I hadn't showered hours ago because I was starting to sweat in all the wrong places. I was particularly concerned about a briefcase that Greg carried in his left hand.

When the elevator doors opened, Jerry stepped out into a thickly carpeted, silent hallway lit by well-spaced sconces and pointed to the left. The other brother started down the hallway with Sally close behind. I lingered long enough to see Jerry lean against the open door of the elevator and cross his arms. It was too late to wish I was somewhere else and definitely too late to have stayed in the car.

At Apartment 1748, Greg stopped and knocked quietly. After a long moment, the door swung partly open and we were greeted by the face of a small, bent and aged dowager who smiled thinly without the slightest hint of recognition of the two standing in the hallway.

"Dorothea!" Sally bubbled enthusiastically, "So great to see you. Do you mind if we come in?"

Dorothea smiled but said nothing. She was clearly confused, especially once Sally pushed the door open the rest of the way and stepped in, taking her by the elbow.

"Let's sit and catch up. Shall we?"

"I'm sorry, who are you again?" Dorothea finally found her voice.

"Why silly, it's me, Margaret. You remember me don't you, from the Art Institute? We were on the board together."

"Oh. I should make tea."

"Don't trouble yourself Dorothea. We only have a minute, but I was in the neighborhood and couldn't let the opportunity pass. How have you been?"

"Well…I guess I've…I've been okay."

I took a place just inside the living room and turned to watch Greg. He went into the kitchen, set his briefcase on the counter and snapped the latches open. Once it was open he lifted out a small pistol grip drill. Turning to the wall above the sink, he tapped a few spots and then began to drill a hole with a long drill bit, just below the bottom of the cabinet. As Sally chattered on in the living room, the little drill barely made a sound doing its work in the drywall. Once done with the first hole, he drilled a second in the bottom of the adjoining cabinet.

I started to wonder if there was a way to induce amnesia because I was going to need it. I was already in over my head, and it was getting progressively more serious by the minute.

Once Greg had the holes done he replaced the drill gun and drew out a long fiber optic chord and what looked like a small camera. He ran the cable into the hole in the wall and then up into the cabinet. Hooking up the camera to the cable, he placed it far back on the shelf. Far enough back so that little Dorothea would not be able to notice it, then closed the cabinet and wiped down the countertop and sink with the sponge from the sink. Turning, he winked at me and smiled. It had taken less than five minutes.

"Ready SQ."

Sally had been sitting with Dorothea while she droned

on about family members, now departed. She quickly rose to her feet and pointed to the wall clock.

"Oh my goodness, look at the time. Now I'll be hopelessly late! It's been so nice catching up Dorothea. We must do it again sometime soon."

"What? You're leaving? Already?"

"Oh dear yes. I'm so late, but I didn't want to pass up the opportunity to see you while I was in town. Good bye my dear." She bent down and gave the old woman a brief hug and then turned and went out the still open front door. "I'll be back soon, I promise."

Once out in the hallway, Greg quickly caught the end of the protruding optic cable and screwed a small lens on the end. Then he fit the lens back into the drilled hole and left it flush with the hallway wall. Stepping back he surveyed the work and nodded. It was almost invisible.

"Now we can see who comes and goes down this hallway." Sally supplied. "It's Bluetooth, but the battery will only last a few days, so we'll have to change it. Dorothea is going to love having someone to talk to again."

At the next apartment going away from the elevator but on the opposite side of the hallway, Greg knocked. Within seconds the door swung open. Quick as a snake, Greg reached in and hauled the person who had opened the door out into the hallway. Straight across the hallway, his face met the solid wall on the other side. He followed that with a very large elbow to the side of the person's head, and as he sagged to the floor, a hard right fist again to the side of the head. The man collapsed in a heap on the floor as Sally stepped by him and into the apartment's open door. It had taken less than ten seconds. As I passed the fallen man, I recognized the fellow I had once met in the entrance alcove at my apartment.

The apartment was a carbon copy of the one we had just left, except this one featured an unobstructed view of the lakefront and across the lake, the twinkling lights of Gary and Michigan City, Indiana on the other side. Lounging in a tracksuit on the oversize sofa was Joseph Battaglia, just beginning to register his surprise at the intrusion.

"You're getting soft Joe. I'd never have gotten in here so easily a few years ago."

"Sa…Sa…Sally?" Recovering quickly, he scooted himself into an erect sitting position, "It's good to see you Sally. You look splendid, as usual."

"Oh Joe, the time for pleasantries is long over. Don't you think?"

"Why are you barging into my house then?"

"You sent a boy to do a man's job Joseph." Sally walked up to him and raising her skirt up to her thigh, she put her high heel right in his crotch. "Apparently, I'm not as easy as you've let yourself become. You should be better than that, or at least you used to be." She leaned on her raised leg and Joe flinched. "This is your only warning, you guinea fucker; stay away or I'll be coming for you old man."

"I don't know what you're talking about."

"Sure you don't."

Battaglia caught movement in his peripheral vision and spied me standing in the hallway.

"So this Fed put you on to me."

"No, but he heard your warning and so did I. I got lucky this time, but seriously, Joe, you've got to do better with your staffing decisions. These guys are fucking useless."

Joe looked over at me.

"So, your true colors come through huh? Teaming up with the Beech's again, just like your daddy. What will they say down at the station house?"

"We don't have a station house."

"Well the FBI usually doesn't hire punk criminals either." He flinched as Sally leaned on her heel again.

"Just this once Joe or the gloves come off. Leave me alone, and just don't fuck with anyone else either. Geez, can't you just stay retired and eat your spaghetti?"

"I apologize Sally for my language, but fuck you."

"Don't fuck with me Joe, that's final." She gave him one more hard nudge in the crotch with her heel and then stepped back from him. "Next time there won't be a warning, capiche?"

Before we left I helped Greg drag the guy in out of the hallway and back into the apartment. He was going to have a whopper of a headache when he finally came to. We pulled the door closed behind him. Jerry hadn't moved from the elevator since we'd left him leaning against the open door. It was ready to go.

Back out on the street, Jerry took the parking valet by the elbow and walked him out to the curb, where he opened his wallet. The valet never noticed the rest of us climbing back into the black SUV.

When we pulled back out into traffic and headed back out of town again, I turned to Sally.

"That wasn't fair Sally."

"Why not? Do you think you can stay self-righteous forever. You needed a little dose of reality."

"Reality usually doesn't include aggravated assault, breaking and entering—twice, and illegal surveillance Sally. You did that on purpose."

"Not really, but I wanted you to know how seriously we take things."

"I already knew that." I huffed a little then turned to her, "He might have been right you know. He might not have known what you were talking about."

"What do you mean by that?"

"He might not have known about the burglar at your house."

"What makes you say that?"

"Because your burglar was Miranda Simonsen's brother."

Sally took a quick deep breath, then looked out the window at the nighttime scenery for a long minute.

"Jerry! I need a drink."

It's My Place

Jerry took a right off Elston Avenue and pulled up in front of what appeared on the outside to be a very busy neighborhood corner tavern. Groups and couples stood on the street corner dressed in chains and leather, smoking more than cigarettes. As soon as the vehicle stopped, Sally stepped out and up the two steps to the entrance of a place simply called, 'The Corner' without the slightest hesitation. With the car in a designated 'No Parking' zone, Jerry and Greg took positions next to the monstrous SUV and faced off the crowd who looked on curiously. Jerry cocked an eyebrow and motioned me to follow Sally in.

Inside heavy metal music was just below the decibel level of the sound barrier. The girl at the front door sported total tattoo sleeves on both arms, looked Sally up and down, and smiled. I cast my eyes around slightly stunned by the impact of the sound and the visual stimulus. The place was packed with a 'standing-room-only' crowd. Everywhere goths, bikers and stoners were intermixed in apparent harmony. Several people exhibited different surgically enhanced body modifications. The bartender sported two perfectly symmetrical devil horn implants and had no visible skin surface that hadn't yet been inked. I liked the place immediately.

"Two seats at the bar?" Sally yelled.

"We're really slammed Mrs. Carlisle; you should go straight back tonight." She yelled back

We followed her meandering hips as she negotiated her way through the throng, oblivious to the press of bodies. The deeper we went into the room, the more crowded it seemed to become. We bypassed the bar completely and then at the back of the saloon, she opened a small door with a key from her pocket and ushered us into a spacious back room with a long, polished office table surrounded by several plush leather office chairs. Sallie immediately shrugged off her fur coat, skirted the table, and took the seat at the far end of the table.

"A martini, please Sara, dry. Whiskey for my friend."

"Yes, ma'am. Will you be dining this evening?"

"Yes. I suppose we should. Would you please bring Mr. Quinn a menu?"

"Of course." She turned to me, "We feature the best burgers in Chicago sir, and we have several whiskeys to draw from Mr. Quinn?"

"Jack Daniels would be fine."

"We have a very good single barrel, will that be suitable?"

"Very!"

"One more thing Sara?"

"Yes Mrs. Carlisle?"

"Have the boys come in as well. Someone else can watch the car I think."

"Yes ma'am."

"No flirting with Greg."

With one last nod to Sally, Sara exited back out into the hubbub and wall of sound, but when the door closed only the lowest sounds and the beat of the bass notes could be felt. I was still standing in my coat. I looked down the table at her as she shrugged.

"I own this place. It's a popular spot, and completely legit. Like a license to print money you might say. I like to keep my hand in a little business now and then. Money doesn't make itself after all."

Later, I pushed back my plate, unable to finish it. The menu had proved completely inscrutable to me, with names that evoked memories of the past but contained no meaningful information about the cuisine. I had finally settled on a selection titled 'Black Sabbath-Paranoid.' It had proved to be easily the best burger I had ever eaten in my life. It had also proved to be my Waterloo; it was too good but I couldn't finish it. I leaned back and finished my drink, wondering if I could loosen my belt in front of all the others.

Both Greg and Jerry had ordered the selection titled Led Zeppelin-Stairway to Heaven. Both had finished theirs in half the time it had taken me not to finish mine. Sally had devoured a monstrous thing and worked her way through a third martini. They had all leaned back in their seats to watch me struggle to finish, but when I had pushed my plate back, Sally pulled out her cell phone and dialed.

"Working tonight? Good. We're on Elston, go 10-92. We'll wait."

I knew better than to ask at this point. My best advice to myself was to act like I'd been there before. I was in way over my head, and I was not skating down the line between good and bad anymore. I tried to justify my actions by reminding myself that it was part of my investigation but even I couldn't fool myself that much.

My own best advice at this point was to just wait and see. A waiter arrived to clear plates, and Sara brought fresh drinks to everyone.

"Sara, we are expecting the police to arrive shortly. Please show them through; I apologize for the interruption. Don't let them linger in the dining room please. Also, bring two tap beers and two shots of Hennessey."

"Yes ma'am."

Within minutes, the door opened and two uniformed patrol officers were ushered into the room. Both officers didn't bluster; instead, they nodded to Greg and Jerry and smiled at Sally.

"Nice to see you Sal." The officer with stripes on his sleeve spoke up, "Where you been?"

"Nice to see you too Danny. How've you been keeping."

"Can't complain. I gotta write you a ticket though Sal. Gotta justify the patrol stop. That okay?"

"No problem, Danny. Leave it on the windshield please. I've got a little problem and I hope you can help me out."

"Not as easy as that. That last favor was hard to sell."

"This one's easy. Enjoy your drinks, and have a seat. I won't keep you long."

Both officers pulled out chairs on opposite sides of the table. Lifting their shot glasses to each other they threw back the drinks and then lifted their beer steins.

"Who's the stiff?" Danny looked at me.

"He's a teammate; no worries Danny."

"He looks like a cop."

"He is a cop, but not on the same street as you. But he's okay."

"I'm not comfortable with another cop in the room Sal."

I reached into my coat pocket and flipped my shield out on the table. Both cops recoiled and Danny pushed away from the table.

"What the hell? Feds?"

"He's on our side, at least for now. We're trying to solve a problem, both his problem and my problem. This is not a big favor Danny, I could ask the same questions about your partner here. He's new isn't he?"

"A rookie. Sid got a disciplinary. He's on leave; doesn't look like he might come back."

"Well teach this one good. First though, he's going to need to learn that if I say the Feds okay, then he's okay."

"Okay Sal, I'm just being careful."

"You should."

"What's the favor?"

"Like I said, this is an easy one."

"Okay, clock's ticking."

"You got a guy down at the lockup. He's a bail jumper, so he's not out yet, but he will be. I don't want anything to happen to him while he's there."

"You think that's likely?"

"Who knows, you guys let Bobby Dey-Dey get killed."

"I didn't have anything to do with that."

"Good, but I don't want anything to happen to this kid. Names Bradley Simonsen."

"Okay. Why?"

"When he gets out, bring him to me. That's all. Just bring him to me. That's all, nothing more."

"Just like that?"

"Just like that." Sally waved her hand, "Finish your beer, but then the clock's ticking. Greg show these guys out, and make sure the visit was worth their while."

Greg pushed back and went to the door. The two cops followed him out. I looked a question at Sally, but Jerry spoke up looking at me.

"You got the narrative wrong."

"What?" I was confused, but also pretty sure I'd never heard Jerry speak before, so I was surprised too.

"Have you looked at the crime scene Tom?" Sally asked.

"Harry's crime scene? Yes, more than once."

"What did it tell you?"

"More questions than answers really."

"Like?"

"I'm not sure that I can share that with you Sally."

"Relax, I have my own copy."

"Oh. Well, for one, both men walked through the crime scene after the initial murders occurred. I thought that was strange."

"Agreed. Anything else?"

"There's one thing, and I'm just kind of stuck on it."

"Like how no one heard the shots?"

"No. It was early morning, but after most people had left for work and it was a smaller caliber weapon. I didn't give any strength to that. No it was something else."

"Like?"

"The gun was a .38 caliber Ruger Security Six revolver. Most of the Rugers have a five shot chamber, but this one has six. All the cartridges in the gun had been fired, but only five of the shots were accounted for. No mention of the missing bullet was noted. I can't understand why that wasn't a point of interest."

"They had been trying to nail Harry on anything for years. He handed them a Class 4 felony on a silver platter. They didn't have any reason to look any further than what was perfectly obvious at the crime scene."

"The stiletto was made by the Jeweler as you know by now. He gave it to Miranda Dugan as a gift, but when I told Harry he had a stroke. Almost literally had a stroke."

"For good reason."

"Why? What do you mean?"

Protege

Sally Carlisle rolled her chair away from the table and reached across to a small button on the wall and pushed it. Within seconds, Sara re-entered the room.

"I'll be needing another drink, and the same all around Sara. Congratulations on a great crowd tonight. Were the cops an interruption for you?"

"Actually no ma'am. We all know those two and don't pay much attention to them when they bother the smokers outside. I think they know better than to fuck with us."

"That's correct. Bring the next round, wait five minutes and bring a second."

"Excuse me?"

"Just indulge me."

After Sara left, there were a couple of minutes of

silence interrupted by Greg returning to the room. This time with a small dark-skinned man. The man arrived reluctantly, and with Greg's gigantic hand on one of his shoulders. Greg steered him into a seat at the foot of the table directly opposite Sally. He looked up at her once, then directed his eyes between his feet.

"Well! Goodness gracious what have we here? Nice to see you again Emilio. Have you been out of town?"

"No." He spoke to his shoes.

"I swear. I asked you a simple question. You told me you would find out about it and get back to me. What happened?"

"I musta forgot."

"You forgot! Really. You forgot your old friend Sally Square. After all we've been through? That can't be true can it?"

"You've got it wrong Sal. The words on the street is Harry's singing to the Feds, so they're saying stay away from Sally Square. I didn't know. I just thought I'd lay low for now and see."

"See who wins, you mean."

"No. Well yeah, I guess."

"Turns out I didn't need your help. I got the Feds to give me what I wanted, so you're off the hook. At least for tonight, but I'm not happy Emilio my friend. Boys would you take Emilio out back and explain to him how unhappy he's made me please?"

With that both Greg and Jerry rose to their feet to the horror of Emilio. Together they lifted him out of his chair, propelled him to the door at the back of the office suite, and then into the alley. The exchange had taken less than two minutes.

Sally casually drained her glass as Sara arrived with a new round of drinks. She smiled at me. "Emilio is one of my ears and eyes on the street. Lately, he's had trouble with his allegiances; he's become less dependable. A little encouragement is better than burning him down altogether. Emilio thinks he's a pretty smart cookie, but his survival instincts are not very good."

I drained my glass and then drained the one that Sara handed me. In no way, was this evening turning out to have career building opportunity written on it. I was getting more nervous by the minute.

"Sally, do you realize how far off the track you're trying to take me?"

"Sara, make the next round a double." She directed a huge smile at me, "Yes…yes I do Tom."

She was interrupted as Jerry and Greg returned through the back door. They were not accompanied by Emilio. Both of them took their usual seats and finished their first drinks then toasting each other with the new ones, drained them as well.

"I know what it is that we're showing you, but I want you to look at it from a slightly different angle. What you do, who you are is governed by very black and white guidelines. They are what we call the law, at least when it is convenient for us. Most of us spend a good deal of our time trying to find ways around the law or a way to make the law work for us, but just us. Nobody else.

"Down here in the street, there is a lot less of the law and a lot more personalities. Everyone has found their way around the particular law that influences their endeavors. No one absolutely adheres to the guidelines of the one true law. Everyone is just trying to get by; there's no room or time for the law or the courts; everyone finds their own way. That's how things get done, you get yours best you can and I get mine best I can, but sometimes we can get at crossed purposes with each other and then we sort it out ourselves. We don't call the police, we don't file a legal suit; we negotiate, we butt heads, but we resolve the issue. That's what you are seeing Tom, how the real world goes around. Now have a drink, relax and see our other side of life."

When Sara returned I was deeply thankful for the double shot in my drink.

Randa

Sally toyed with her drink glass, slouching back in her chair, she swirled it and ran her finger around the rim. It had become very quiet, and the sounds from out in the bar seemed to fade even to a greater degree. Finally, she reached out and opened her beaded clutch purse and took out a cigarette case. After selecting one, she lit it and took a long puff. She took two or three more, then reached across and took one of Jerry's empty beer bottles, dropped the half-smoked remainder into it, and gave it a shake. Replacing the bottle on the table she spoke directly to it instead of the rest of us in the room.

"He used to call her his little mascot. She was so cute. She followed him everywhere."

"Sara?"

Sally chuckled, "No Tom, we were talking about Randa, Miranda Simonsen, remember? She was one-hundred percent Harry's little mascot."

"Seriously?"

"Seriously. She was a petty thief in the early days and not a very good one. She kept getting caught and it was just a matter of time before she would have ended up in Juvie. She couldn't have been more than thirteen or fourteen back then. That's when she ran up against Harry for the first time. She was mostly stealing food and necessities, things young women at that age suddenly need, if you know what I mean."

"I guess. How did she meet Harry?"

"Harry kept an eye on businesses that had protection agreements. If he had negotiated a contract to make sure businesses weren't victimized, then Harry took it seriously and kept an eye on all of them personally. He was in a store one day and watched Randa doing her best. He told me later it was all he could do not to laugh out loud. But he snagged her and took her outside, gave her a good lecture and probably a smack upside the head too. Then he made her go back into the store and pay for what she had tried to steal with money that he gave her to do it.

"After that Randa took to following Harry around. She started turning up wherever he was. As cute as it was, there were things and people that Harry didn't want to be seen with. Especially, someone he didn't think he could trust. So it wasn't all that cute to Harry. Randa was persistent though and eventually Harry started sending her on errands, little jobs, delivering messages, stuff like that. It was probably her first paying job and she tried to do it well. As the jobs got more complicated, she needed an appearance upgrade. Harry brought Randa to me for wardrobe and hygiene lessons.

"When we got the dirt and grime scrubbed off of her, it was an incredible revelation. She was absolutely beautiful, not just a beautiful teenager, she was beautiful by anyone's standard at any age. She was tall, a little too skinny but with a figure just the same. She had long blond hair, perfect teeth and the bluest eyes you've ever seen. She had the full arsenal and she was smart too.

"I offered to have her move in with me once Harry made it clear that she was becoming more and more valuable, but she wouldn't have it. She insisted on going home every night, no matter how late he kept her out, but she'd be back the next day when the sun came up. She didn't seem to go to school or have connections to others in the community, but she adored Harry. And Harry returned the affection, he doted on her and the jobs got tougher, as I understand it. When she turned eighteen, Harry put her to work in earnest. She had a knack for it, the dating and the ability to get people talking to her. She could get more information out of a man after a couple drinks than Harry could get in six months of wining and dining. She became Harry's signature piece."

Sally stopped and popped open her purse again. She took out the cigarette case and held it in her hand for a moment, then made a decision and put it back into her purse again.

"One night, I don't remember when exactly, Randa was to have dinner with a new client of Harry's. The guy apparently misunderstood the guidelines for the evening and forced himself upon her or tried anyway. Randa defended herself, she was a street girl, she knew how things worked on the street, so when I say she defended herself, what I mean is—she killed him.

"Afterward, she called Harry. According to him, the crime scene was a total mess. He had to call in a couple of favors to get it cleaned up. Bobby Dey-Dey was probably one of them. Then he brought Randa to my place. Every stitch of clothing on that girl was bloody. She had fought with him at the same time that she was stabbing him with a steak knife. Her clothes were a mess, but Miranda Sorensen was unfazed by the event. She was not panicked, she was not distraught, she wasn't even nervous. She was like ice."

"Jeez!"

"She got better at it though. Not so messy." Jerry leaned back in his chair and looked across at me, "She got way better."

"She worked at it. She came to me for etiquette, wardrobe and language. She took self-defense classes, studying karate and jiu jitsu, and she…"

"Wait a minute! You trained her to be an assassin? An eighteen-year-old girl?"

"No! We trained her to be a lady."

"But you knew she killed that guy."

"Yes."

"Killing people is considered not just illegal Sally, it's generally accepted as bad behavior."

"We didn't encourage her Tom, but her job working for Harry could have been dangerous. She was getting busier and busier as Harry's protégé. She was making very good money. She had become her own person and controlled her own fate so to speak. She and Harry were a hard team to get past. She started carrying a knife."

"That's crazy! How many people did she kill?"

"Harry knows."

"But what happened? She was a mom when she was killed."

"Jack Dugan happened. Handsome and clever." Both nephews snorted. "He got under her skin, she couldn't get enough of him, and he promised her everything and heaven itself." Again the nephews both snorted. "So she went to Harry and told him she wanted out."

"Just like that?"

"Just like that. By that time Harry and Randa trusted each other completely. Harry knew Randa wouldn't spill any information, she was as good with secrets as he was, so he let her go. I'm sure it practically killed him. They were close, like the perfect daughter that he never had. In the end, he let her go and she moved to the west side and became a mom."

"But it didn't last."

"No. Jack Dugan wanted more. The life they'd put together wasn't exciting or interesting enough for him. He wanted to be included in the inner circles. The trouble was, he couldn't be trusted. He talked to anybody and everybody. Who he knew, what he knew and most of all who he was going to be someday. So Jack Dugan was all he was ever going to be, a legend in his own mind but not even a glimmer of interest on anyone else's radar."

"So he left her?"

"I don't know but I doubt it. Randa would have taken as much as she wanted and then she probably threw him out. He may have been the man in that relationship, but Randa would have been the one wearing the pants."

"I couldn't talk to that guy for more than five minutes

before I wanted to shove my fist through his face." Greg snarled

"Same," said Jerry

"You knew the guy?"

"Randa dragged him around like a personal boat anchor. We all met him; no one liked him."

"What happened to him?"

"He went to work back downtown. Hanging out with the wrong people and doing shit jobs. Haven't heard anything about him in quite a while now. Good riddance."

"So Brad Sorensen said that Miranda went to Harry and asked for her old job back."

"She did?" The surprise in Sally's voice was clear.

"That's what he said."

"That's odd. She didn't need the money, I know that. The house was paid for, and she was smart with money. She'd put away plenty over the years, so she couldn't have needed money and I know Jack didn't take any with him."

"Maybe she just missed the excitement?"

"Once you get clear of that lifestyle it's never a good idea to try and get back in. Almost never works out for the best. Harry would have been pretty clear about that, but you should ask him."

"It almost killed him last time."

"He'll be better prepared this time."

Sic'em Tom!

I was hunkered down at my desk chair clasping my paper coffee cup in both hands. I was hungover, and maybe still just a little drunk, but most definitely still hungover after my evening with Sally the night before. I was staring into the abyss of absolutely nothing at the bottom of my cup until the SAC leaned into my cubicle. He gave me a critical look.

"Good morning probie! You look like death warmed over."

"Late night," I mumbled.

"Ah, to be young and single again. C'mon you're riding with me today. You can give me all the lurid tales on the way. Get your gear checked out. Let's go!"

"Go?"

"Joint task force. We've got a cell to take down. ATF,

SWAT and us, c'mon now Tom the briefing was just last week. Get your shit together."

"Oh…oh yeah, I just forgot. I'll be right there."

"I'll be down at the car. We can talk on the way. Your report from last week is a little light on details."

"That's it?!" The SAC diligently negotiated the rush hour traffic as we wove through the South Side streets.

"Honest Chief, he mostly sleeps these days. I haven't talked much to him all last week. He did give up the Mencorini thing though."

"Lean in on it a little Tom. He's getting close and it's the fourth quarter."

"I asked him about the sixth bullet."

"Oh yeah? What did he have to say about that?"

"Nothing. He blew me off."

"I told you it was nothing. Leave it and start putting the screws to him."

When we pulled up to the staging area, our crew was out in the parking lot strapping on their Kevlar vests, clearing weapons and checking hand radios at the back of their vehicles; all the trunk lids were up. "Pay attention now Tom, let SWAT do the heavy lifting. We're here to make the arrests, not the sweaty stuff. No heroes today. Understand?"

"Yes sir."

I grabbed my vest and met the others behind the SAC's sedan.

"Well look who's here." "Where you been probie?" "I don't know Johnny should we even let him have a gun?"

"Shuddup you guys."

"How's your mystery man? He dead yet? Nice you could join us—for a change." It was all good natured, just guy talk welcoming me to the crew.

"Can it you guys." The SAC came around the rear end of the car struggling into his own vest. "Arm yourself Tom. I'm going to look for the AIC. You guys chill out until I get back."

"How you been doin' Tom?" Bob English looked earnestly at me. Bob had been an agent since before I had gone to kindergarten. He was a hard core veteran, but he also had been the most welcoming at the bureau. Today he looked me in the eye and saw more than just a hangover.

I returned the look and shrugged. "Okay, I guess."

"Tough duty. Gotta be. Watchin' a guy die on the installment plan."

"Tell me about it."

"What's he like? Tough guy like that; he can't be going easy-like. He fightin' it?"

"Surprisingly, he's at peace. Or sort of anyway."

"What d'ya mean, 'at peace'?"

"He doesn't seem to care. It's like he's watching it happen to himself, but only as an observer. He's detached from the process, but definitely paying attention."

"That's fucked up."

"You have no idea."

"RUNNER! RUNNER! Northeast, heading northeast!" The staticky message came across our 'com' link units.

I looked up just as everyone else did. If the message was true, he was heading right for us. As we watched, all of us saw the flicker of motion as an individual vaulted a backyard fence and hit the ground running. After another hundred feet up the alley the runner looked up and saw us all watching him, waiting for his arrival. He stopped dead in his tracks in a spray of gravel and sand. He then turned ninety degrees and sprinted away between the two garages facing out into the alley, and out of sight.

"Get him probie!' Sic 'em!"

I didn't even consider it. I dropped the rifle back into the open trunk and bolted away from them. When I got to where I had last seen him, I immediately spied him moving cautiously across the backyard of the house belonging to the garage in the alley. He heard me before he saw me and took off at a dead run. I fixated on the perp's retreating back; he had a good lead; he looked fast, and I was hungover. I tried to pick up speed and I was suddenly angry. Furious with this fucked up life where I had to chase some useless motherfucker when my head hurt this bad. Angry at the shit detail where I was supposed to do my job with a dead man and like it. I kicked my speed up a notch and gained on him. The madder I got, the faster I got. When he had trouble vaulting the next yard's fence, I cut the distance in half. As angry as I might ever have been, I cleared the fence in a single vault and was on him before he crossed the next yard.

"Slow down motherfucker!"

After tackling him to the ground, I wrestled him prone. I should have cuffed him, but then I was still just a little drunk, still angry and definitely still hungover. I was gasping for breath but had to admit that I felt somewhat better about myself. I was still straddling him and rolled him over to face me and get a better look at him. He came up with a gun and fired point blank. The bullet caught me in my right armpit above my vest and burned like fire. I was so lit up with the adrenalin of the chase that I never hesitated. I grabbed the hot barrel of the revolver in my right hand and punched him in the face with my left hand. He immediately let go of the gun, and I punched him in the face with it too.

"You have the right to remain silent!" I punched him in the face.

"Anything you say can and will be held against you in a court of law!" I began punching him a few more times with the pistol.

"You have a right to an attorney, if you cannot afford an …."

That's when they pulled me off of him.

"Easy Quinn! Easy. Shit you can't do that to the perp man!"

"I read him his rights." I panted, struggling to resume my endeavors.

"Man! You can't assault someone like that."

Multiple arms lifted me into a standing position but I suddenly couldn't stand on my own anymore. I needed to rest. My knees wouldn't hold me up anymore and I tried to lie down, maybe for just a minute.

"Wait! Is that…blood? Shit, he's bleeding. Shit! Shots fired! Shots fired! Officer down. Repeat! Officer down."

I watched as the ambulance's flashing lights reflected off the buildings we passed by. It turns out that karma is really a bitch after all.

Rehab

The next week had been spent as a guest at one of Chicago's finest trauma care centers with a tube sticking out of my chest. I had a collapsed right lung, pneumothorax, whatever that is, and a different appreciation for the value of human life, especially mine.

Even though the bullet had made a comparatively small hole in me, my whole body hurt. It hurt to move and it hurt to lie still. And most of all, it hurt to think about the mess I had landed myself in. There had been chances along the way for me to back away from the situation, but now it felt too late. By acting like a complete rookie and trying to please everyone, I managed to paint myself into a corner that had real consequences. I was going to recover from being shot, but once I was back out on the street, I was too far down the rabbit hole to find my way back out. At least not without getting shot again, or losing my job, or both.

It was not a healthy situation for physical or mental recovery. Not only had being shot been a classically rookie mistake, but I had also succeeded in creating a schizophrenic life situation. The time had passed for me to walk into the SAC's office and confess my sins. Even if there was a chance that I could somehow tell the story in my very best light, there was still the little matter of my father's criminal background that would color any story I could concoct.

Conversely, Sally Carlisle had begun to demonstrate an extended reach. I was fascinated by her and more than a little frightened of her. No doubt she would take a jaundiced view of any report that I might fabricate. The current list of her felonious activities would be hard to understate, but I was also fairly certain that, somehow, none of the various crimes would stick. She had already demonstrated that she could carry a grudge.

Through all of it, the nurses and therapist were diligent, if not entirely compassionate and definitely not sympathetic to my foul mood. I was not abusive; that would have made me feel even worse. If I was being completely honest with myself, I would have admitted that I was wallowing in self-pity. I did the exercises and took their pills but didn't do it with a smile on my face. It came as no surprise to anyone on the staff that no one came to visit during my stay. After six days, they sent me home with a little plastic 'good-bye' baggie, filled with well wishes, directions for multiple medications and emergency numbers in case an unexplained bleeding incident should occur. When I had inquired what an 'unexplained' bleeding incident might be, the nurse hedged and was uncertain. So I asked her if getting shot again might be an unexplained bleeding incident.

She cocked an eyebrow at me and said, "No. After the week I've just spent with you, there are going to be plenty of people that are gonna want to shoot you. You better get used to that." Which hurt my feelings a little.

I got a ride home from the bureau guys. They were nice, apologetic. Most of them had never been shot before. I almost felt like they were a little jealous, I guess.

I tried staying home and resting but lived in a second-floor walkup studio apartment above a pizza parlor. Except for street traffic, there was nothing to see, nothing to look at and nothing to do. You can only surf the internet so many hours of the day. I began to lose my mind in less than a week and reported back for duty. I could rehab while I sat watching Harry die. It would be like watching paint dry; the view was only marginally better than out of my apartment windows, but I would be doing something.

The Chief was skeptical, gave me a sympathetic nod, but then reminded me that it was a wonder that Harry was still alive.

The first day back it seemed that I had not remembered how long the walk was from the front gate into the bowels of the jail and the ward where they kept Harry. By the time I arrived at the infirmary suite, I was panting for breath and for the first time, I eased down into the chair in the corner, grateful that it was there. I caught my breath and looked over at him. His black eyes looked back.

"Heard you got shot." He rasped.

"Yeah? Who'd you hear that from?"

"Fuck you."

"Yeah, I got shot. Sorry I missed a couple weeks Harry. How're you doing?"

"Fuck you care?"

"You know something Harry? I get it. Couple of weeks ago, I thought I'd bought it. The real deal. I get it. It's not funny."

"It is funny though—in a way."

"How so?"

"It's inevitable. But we pretend it isn't until that point where we can't deny it anymore. Then we begin to repent."

"Repent for our sins." I nodded.

"No! We repent for the opportunities that we missed. The doors we should have walked through."

"Isn't that funny now that you say that. I spent some time while I was staring at the ceiling in the hospital wishing I'd asked Karen Havelhorst out back in high school."

"Missed opportunity, not sin. That's what we regret. If we had the opportunity for sin we would most likely do it again, but if we had the opportunity of a lifetime right in front of us, we would probably miss it again, I promise. We hate ourselves for it. But the clock only turns forward, never backward, so there is only the regret."

"Do you regret anything Harry?"

"They have elevated my pain medications today." He took a long breath in through his nose and let it out slowly through his mouth. "I'd almost decided that you would not be coming back, but here you are. I am in a fairly comfortable state for the moment and to be honest, I feel like a bit of conversation Thomas." He rearranged the bed sheet and then gave me a slight smile. "But don't get your hopes up."

"I have some regrets. I'm still not too sure about the FBI decision to be honest. That would be a big regret."

"You are hopelessly young yet. Although the last couple weeks has added a few years of maturity I'd wager."

"I've been shot before Harry."

"But this time was different. You were doing it for your job and you fucked up. No way you should get shot if you're doing it by the numbers. You weren't doing it because you loved your country, for the 'good ol' U.S. of A. You get paid to do your job. This time you did it for the money and you fucked up somehow. You start to wonder if you got your money's worth."

"No, no. It wasn't like that. I did it for some other reason."

"Like?"

"I don't know. I was so mad. It was nuts. I wanted that guy to pay, you know pay for everything I couldn't manage in my life."

"Like?"

"Like you for one thing, asshole!"

"Finally."

"Finally?"

"I can imagine what it's like, sitting there day after day. You've been told to get the dirt from me and you know you never will. You knew you wouldn't get it by about the third visit, but here we are in…what are we at now eight-nine weeks?"

"Ten."

"Ten weeks! I bet you didn't think I would take so long when you first started all of this, did you?"

"It's irrelevant."

"I suppose." Harry reached down and pushed the call button on his bed. Taking his arm out from under the blanket, one thing became immediately clear. His handcuff had been removed.

"When did they take the handcuff off?"

"When I promised not to do anything that would get them into trouble. I'm a man of my word and they know it."

We were interrupted when Roberto, the day nurse, bustled into the room.

"You rang Mr. Beech?"

"Yes, I believe it's time for my next dose. Could I please have it?"

"It's actually not time yet Harry, but I'll be right back."

By this time, I had gotten familiar with Harry's facial expressions, or the usual lack thereof. Today I took another critical look and saw the tightness of his lips and the bulging muscles of his jawline.

"Does it hurt much Harry?"

"Over the last week, the damn thing has found a new place inside of me to invade. This one is the mother lode. It has my almost undivided attention."

Roberto returned and busied himself with Harry's IV. As he slowly administered the pain medication, Harry let out a deep sigh and his head dropped back on the pillow. Within seconds his eyes lost their focus and his entire body went limp. Roberto finished the dosage and raised his eyebrows at me before he left.

"That's all he gets for the next four hours. It's already a high dose, but we can raise it even higher if he asks for it."

"What do you think Roberto?" I didn't have to say what I was really asking him.

"I think it will be this week."

"I do too." Harry whispered

For the next three days I sat in that uncomfortable chair in the corner and watched Harry sleep. I watched as the four-hour window for medication approached and he became increasingly agitated. He would shift his position and struggle to turn, only to turn back the other way in seconds. Only semi-conscious he flailed his arms and sighed over and over. Once he had received his next dose of morphine, he would sigh and slide back into unconsciousness, barely breathing, his sightless eyes partially open, only the blips on the screen showing the suppressed signs of life still there.

On the fourth day, as I approached his glassed room, I was surprised to see others in the room ahead of me and the door braced open. Standing next to Harry's bed was the doctor, his stethoscope in place as he listened to his chest. Extra chairs had been brought in from the hallway and arranged around Harry's bed. Even my plastic monster had been moved out from the corner.

Two of the chairs were occupied. Sitting in them were a couple of elderly inmates, easily identifiable in their orange jumpsuits. I stood in the doorway taking in the sight and watching the doctor finish his examination and then nod to me.

"He's refusing his pain medication today," Roberto spoke to me over my shoulder. "He said he wants to talk to you guys without it."

"Is this okay? The visitors I mean?"

"The doctor cleared it." He gave a long sigh, "It's not going to be long now."

Harry raised his chin from his chest and his eyes focused on me.

"C'mon in. You got a front-row seat Thomas." He croaked.

"I'll be back after I do my other rounds Harry." The doctor placed a hand on Harry's chest for emphasis, "Please Harry, take the morphine."

"Can't yet Doc, things to do."

"I'll be back in a little while, but I think you're making a mistake."

"Just one in a lifetime of them Doc."

The doctor backed out of the room and pulled it shut behind him. In the silence that ensued, the little robot wheezed quietly and the screens on the gantry blipped. I was still standing at the foot of the bed, not sure what I should be doing but fully appreciating the implications of the situation.

"Have a seat Tom. These are my friends Irving and Lester." Harry waved a hand in their direction. "Guys, make nice. Introduce yourselves."

Both of them remained seated but offered a handshake. I eased past them and took the empty seat near the head of the bed.

"Don't sit there Thomas; I can't turn my head that far."

We all slid and scraped our chairs toward the foot, so we could see him face on.

"I have a few things to say that I can't say once they

give me the meds. I wanted you guys to be here because you've been good friends when I didn't have any others. I'm glad you're here too Thomas, it's almost the end of your detail, and you've been anything if not diligent."

He readjusted his position turning slightly toward us and waved one hand vaguely toward me.

"Thomas if you would. There are a few letters here under my pillow. Would you take them out? Let me see them. Yes, the top one. If you would open it and read it out loud for us please. The others are addressed already and I would appreciate it if you would hand-deliver them when you get the chance. They're for people you know, so it shouldn't be a chore."

The stationary was thickly bonded, and the logo on the corner of the envelope was from a law firm with an expensive Michigan Avenue address. Inside was a one-page letter written under the firm's impressive masthead. I started to scan the page, but Harry stopped me.

"Read it out loud Tom."

"There's an address, and the letter is written to you Harry. It reads:

> Dear Mr. Beech,
>
> As your attorney law firm for last twenty-seven years, it has always been our pleasure and privilege to represent you and your interests. As per your instructions, we have completed your most recent requests and are pleased to inform you that we believe that we have resolved the situations most favorably. We hope that you will be happy with the results.

In the matter of Lester Stephens, we have petitioned the courts and prison board at your request. Our application for compassionate release on a probationary basis based on exemplary behavior and citizenship while incarcerated has been submitted and approved. Mr. Stephens will be released to a transitionary halfway house for a period of six months and then fully released pending a successful performance on his part. This release to begin effectively on the first of May of this calendar year.

In the matter of Irving Joyce, we have petitioned the courts and prison board in a separate request. Our application for compassionate release on a probationary basis based on exemplary behavior and citizenship while incarcerated has been submitted and approved. Mr. Joyce will be released to a transitionary halfway house for a period of six months and then fully released under similar performance standards as Mr. Stephens. This release to begin effectively on the tenth day of May of this calendar year.

During the probationary period, the individuals will be encouraged to locate and secure gainful employment, and meet the requirements of reporting and responsible living. As per your instructions, individual trust accounts have been initiated, and both Lester Stephens and Irving Joyce will receive monthly stipends for living expenses. Funds will be deposited into personal accounts to which they will be given access. Funds will be deposited on the first day of each month in perpetuity or until such time that they may no longer require them.

Again, if there are any further requests please do not hesitate to contact us at your earliest convenience. As always, it is a pleasure to work with you.

Sincerely,

J. John Rathcoate, Esq."

"What the hell Harry! You got us out?"

"Is this for real? Can't be; you're shittin' us Harry. C'mon we've been nothin' but nice to you. Don't fuck with us."

"You guys better start thinking about packing. You're getting out; this is a real letter. Harry's done you guys a real solid." I handed Irving the letter and raised my eyebrows at the smiling Harry.

"For real? I'm getting out?"

"Yes," Harry actually managed another small smile, "Somebody's got to get out of here, and it sure isn't gonna be me."

"My fucking god! Thanks Harry. How'd you do it?"

"My motto, 'Stick to business, do what needs to be done but always have a very good lawyer.'"

"What's stipend mean?" Irving was re-reading the letter.

"It means that you're going to be paid once a month, whether you work or not, there will be money put in the bank that is yours to spend any way you like." I answered as Harry nodded.

"No fucking shit?!"

"Yes. Now boys, I need to say a couple of things to Thomas here so we'll need our privacy." Harry pushed a button on the bed rail and raised himself into a more upright sitting position, "but first I need your promise. Actually from all three of you."

"Sure Harry."

"If it ever comes up, I need you guys to protect my reputation. Have any of you ever heard me give anyone up. To anyone?"

"Nope." "No way" "I wish."

"I've kept my secrets, and I intend to take them with me. If it ever comes up, I want you to say just that. Please."

"You've got it Harry."

"No problem Harry, you've always been solid."

"What about you Tom?"

"I can certainly say you've never given me anything I can use."

"So be it. Now if you guys would give us a minute."

Both inmates fell over themselves bowing, nodding and slapping each other on the back, as they carried their chairs back out into the hallway and closed the door behind them. Then Irving burst back into the room for a moment and reached into his pocket; he pulled out two small plastic encased name tags and tossed them onto the bed, smiled and waved as the door snapped shut behind him.

"That was a very nice thing you did Harry."

Harry adjusted his position and winced.

"Why not take the pain medication Harry?"

"Are you kidding?" He gasped, "Why would I do that?"

"Because you're in pain. Even I can see that."

"Boy, you got that right. This hurts like a bitch!"

"So take the medication Harry."

The monitor on the gallows behind the bed showed his rapid breathing and elevated heart rate in alarmingly high numbers and with each read out, the numbers continued to rise.

"No way. This is the last thing that I'm ever going to feel. This is the last feeling that I will ever have. Ever. As bad as it is, why would I cheat myself out of the experience?"

"I never thought of it that way. But I'm sorry that you are suffering."

"I'm not like a dog that just got hit by a car and has a broken leg. You would put the dog out of its misery." He flinched and gasped, then tightened up his jaw and the muscles in his arms stood out with the effort as he grasped the rails of his bedside. "They won't do that for me. Instead they put me to sleep with morphine and hope I die before I wake up. Over and over again until eventually I'm not their problem anymore."

"But c'mon Harry. This is bad."

"Fucking right it is."

"Then why?"

"Because there is no justice."

"What?"

Harry pulled himself up into a sitting position with his

arms on the bed railings and leaned toward me. In a desperate whisper, "C'mon dumbass, you're a smart guy. Find the sixth bullet Tom." He gasped and twitched, "You'll get your answer." He couldn't catch his breath as he struggled for it. Finally, he whispered, "It's the answer to all of it."

His grip on the bed rails relaxed and he sagged back onto the pillow. Multiple alarms beeped and pinged simultaneously. The gallows behind the bed flashed little green and red lights. In response, Roberto burst into the room and pushed a few buttons on the gantry. The alarms stopped and the little green line trembled and then leveled off. The doctor hurried back into the room, his stethoscope ready, but I already knew. I stepped out into the hallway and looked down at my shoes.

"Time of death, four oh seven p.m." The doctor intoned consulting his watch as he lifted the stethoscope off of the still form on the bed.

The cold spring rain was unrelenting. The downpour struck the open umbrellas of all those gathered creating a racket that drowned out the priest's benediction. Try as he might, there were no souls to be saved that day, even if they could have heard him. The meandering roadways of Graceland Cemetery were filled equally with long black sedans and tricked out 'street rides.' Their passengers had emptied out on foot while their drivers remained with the vehicles watching the other drivers. Once the mourners had gathered, they stood separated marginally but together for this final chapter at the graveside, each making sure that they were there to be seen by the others, each making their own homage and statement.

I did not know what kind of event I had imagined it would be. I thought perhaps just Sally Carlisle, Greg and Jerry Beech, but this was not at all what I had expected. There were more than fifty vehicles, each with multiple mourners, some dressed in high-fashioned black and some arrayed in their 'street colors.' Every one of them the elite class of the illegal side of society. The royalty had all turned out, and everyone made it a point to see if the other had shown up. Joseph Battaglia stood in the front row with his two shadows. Close to him, but not too close, Salvatore 'Solly D' DeLaurentis, head of the Chicago Outfit, stood without a hat or an umbrella, hands crossed in front of him. Almost within touching distance a group in the black and gold colors of the Vice Lords stood sunglasses in place and their heads on a swivel. Directly across the grave from them stood their sometimes rivals, sometimes allies in the blacks and reds of the Latin Kings. As we stood there in the rain, I caught more than a few glances in my direction. I was still trying to get used to being an object of interest, and especially by so many with knives in their pockets.

Walking back to the bureau car, the chief caught up with me. "Wow! Tough crowd."

"For sure."

"They're looking at you Tom."

"I don't know anything."

"They don't know that."

"So?"

"So, I think it's time to take a few weeks off. You've not used your rehab time. Take it now. And maybe get out of town for a few days even."

"I don't have anywhere to go."

"Well anywhere would be better for you right now as long as it's not here."

"Thanks Chief, I didn't ask for this."

"I know. But here we are. I don't want to lose my newest agent so I'm instructing you to take a two-week leave. Starting now."

"I can take care of myself sir. Where would I be safer than at the FBI bureau? Wouldn't that make the most sense?"

"Oh come on. It's for your own good."

"When I wanted time off you wouldn't give it to me. Now when I don't want it, you're telling me that I have to."

"I want you one-hundred percent when I have you. You've been seriously injured, you're tired and you're stressed out. Right now you're the next best thing to useless to me. Cripes, you've only been with us for a few months, and you've already gotten more mileage on you than half of the rest of the guys. Take the time; go lay in the sun somewhere. I'll see you in a couple weeks."

"Great."

"But if you run into trouble, pick up a phone. Clear?"

"Count on it."

Count On It!

I slammed the brakes on the car and threw open the door. Throwing my weight into the driver's side door, it sprang open and I landed on the ground on my left shoulder and fired the twelve-gauge shotgun two-handed from under the car door. The fired slug hit the open driver's side door of the stalled vehicle in front of me. Rolling to my left again, I fired in through the windshield and then leaped to my feet. I drew my Glock and held it two-handed out in front of me as I advanced. From my right a man appeared brandishing an assault rifle. I drew center-mass and fired three rounds and paused as he went down. With my head on a swivel I stepped forward, carefully moving from one place of cover to the next. Ahead of me another person appeared shielding something, I took aim but then suddenly they revealed an infant in their arms. I pulled up my aim barely able to prevent pulling the hair trigger.”

“Clear!”

“Clear!”

I cleared my weapon and held the magazine and open handgun up for inspection.

“No brass, no ammo?”

“Clear.”

I paused and reflected, looking out at the tactical range. My pulse slowly ticked back toward normal. I holstered the Glock and entered the range shed.

“You’re slipping Quinn. You missed that first fire, but at least you killed the car.”

“Very funny.”

“Don’t you get tired of coming out here? This is the third time in the last two weeks and your score is always the same. Why don’t you take a break?” He heaved a deep sigh, “Shit, I’m tired of your stupid face and believe me you’ve more than qualified.”

“I’m on leave; I need the practice.”

“You’ve scored 100%, 100% and 97% the last three times out. I’m not going to be your daily source of recreation here, I’ got a job and it ain’t entertainin’ you just because you’re bored. I cut you some slack because of your rehab but do me a favor, don’t come back until your next quarterly qualification.” He looked me full on in the face and narrowed his eyebrows, “And, just so you know, that’s not a request.”

“Fuck.”

Refraction

"So?"

Sally crossed her arms and rested them on the counter in front of her, a martini glass balanced in her left hand. One of the envelopes Harry left with me had been addressed to her. Now it lay on the counter near her elbow, a two-page handwritten letter and what appeared to be a cashier's check. She had read the letter while sipping out of her glass and alternately frowning and at other times, raising her eyebrows in what looked like surprise. At one point she looked up at me for a brief moment before returning to the letter.

"So?"

"Harry's gone and there's nothing we can do about it."

"I know; it's not like I've never had anybody die

before. This just feels different somehow."

"Different how?" She took a sip out of the martini glass and wiggled her head at me.

I looked over her shoulder at the sun-setting light entering through the kitchen windows behind her and tried to put my thoughts into words. The early spring evening light leaning toward hopefulness didn't help my confusion. I looked back into her face and thought I saw honest concern.

"It just seemed like there was so much more. You know? I almost didn't care if it would make any difference to what I was there for in the first place." I stopped and took a considerable mouthful of my drink, "I just wanted to hear the story, his story. I wanted him to make himself—you know—three-dimensional. I just wanted to, you know, to learn more about Harry."

"Then you missed the point of the lesson, didn't you?"

I was shocked and it must have looked so in my face because she smiled and raised her hand in a toast.

"What do you mean?" I took a drink of my own.

"Harry was the most three-dimensional person you might ever meet. What you saw and what he was were as plain as night and day to most people. But who Harry really was, was layers and layers of three-dimensionality deep. Harry was two different people on two different levels depending on what he wanted you to see."

"I knew he was more than what he wanted me to believe he was, but he didn't have anything to prove. He could've come clean with me."

"Tom; Geez! I'm his, or at least I was, his sister. We never talked business. Probably the last time we did might have been the last time I dug a bullet out of him."

"You did that more than once?"

Sally toasted me with her glass and took a sip.

"Well, one way or the other I have to move on. Tomorrow I report back to the bureau, my two weeks of standing around with my hands in my pockets will be over. Maybe I'll be able to get back to work now."

"To do what?"

"I'm sure they'll have something relatively mundane for me to do, at least until I get my shit together anyway."

"That's it?"

"Well, Harry gave me a hint that I could work on too. He wouldn't elaborate, but he hinted."

Sally put down her glass and leaned forward, "What kind of hint?"

"I'm not sure. I just need to think about it a little more before I'm ready to let it go."

"What is it Tom? Did he tell you anything that you didn't already know?"

"No, but it feels important to me. I don't even know why."

"C'mon Tom, what is it?" Sally got up and paced a circle, "I've never heard of Harry hinting at anything that he wouldn't just come right out and say."

"Well this time he didn't say anything. At least anything that I think would be helpful. He was in so much pain at the end, unbelievable really, that he couldn't even speak."

"But what did he say Tom?" Sally leaned back on the counter with both hands.

"Nothing really. It's nothing, just a circular comment."

"Anything Harry would say would be important. It must have been important. What was it?"

Sally's posture was no longer languid relaxation, instead she was tense and as she leaned across the counter, her eyes stared intensely into mine. Her intensity was so different than only minutes before, I reconsidered my casual remarks.

"He talked about his attorney and how important he had been in his life. Apparently, the two of them had been working together for almost three decades. It made me wonder how many secrets he had shared with Rathcoate."

"Rathcoate? Who's that?"

"That was Harry's attorney. He has an office up on the pricey side of the Loop. He said he had been with him for almost thirty years."

"I've never heard of him before. Is that all?"

"Pretty much." I could not explain why I suddenly didn't want to tell her about Harry's last words. I felt they were deeply personal, and he'd only meant them for me. I finished my drink and stood up.

"Time to go?"

"Time to go I think. I'll figure it all out—eventually."

Sally walked me to the front door but before I could step out, she placed a hand on my shoulder.

"It means a lot to me that you were with Harry at the end Tom. Thank you for being his friend and mine. Once this all settles down we'll all be a lot more relaxed."

"It has been more than a little interesting, that's for sure."

"Come back soon Tom."

It was not late enough to be fully dark, but I was tired. It had been a difficult two weeks since Harry had died and I was exhausted with thinking about what Harry had suggested and at the same time looking over my shoulder.

Lost in thought and only partially engaged in driving, I was three blocks from home before I noticed the car following me, again.

Pizza To Go

I noticed the car the first time because it was a nice car. A bright red late model Mercedes-Benz, AMG that stood out in traffic and turned heads. It would have been hard to miss. The kind of car that advertised high income coupled with insecure testosterone issues. It popped up in my rearview mirror yesterday while I was running errands. Later in the day, I'd noticed it again a few cars behind me while I drove south on Lake Shore Drive. It was not a common vehicle, and twice in twenty-four hours was an unlikely coincidence even in a city as big as Chicago.

When I'd gone to Sally's tonight, it appeared again as I wove my way through her neighborhood outside of town. Now it was there again, a polite distance behind me, but there none the less.

I tested my theory by detouring down a narrow side street. Before I made a whole block, it turned down the same street. The driver was making no particular effort to go unnoticed. I meandered my way back to my apartment but instead of looking for a parking spot within walking distance, I turned right on Belmont. Driving directly into the blinding light of the setting sun, I pulled up in front of the building. The pizza joint downstairs was already doing a brisk dinner hour business, and the spot in front was reserved for order pick-ups, and delivery vehicles. I put on my emergency flashers and stepped out of the car, watching for the Mercedes in my peripheral vision. When the following car turned the corner, the driver's hand came up to shield their eyes from the sun. He didn't see my parked car until he had almost passed it. He braked and then looked sideways toward me and we made eye contact. I didn't recognize him, had never seen him before. The car moved on down the street and turned at the next intersection.

There was no way that I was going up into my apartment knowing that I was being stalked. There was only one way out once I was in there. Instead, I pushed my way into the pizza joint downstairs and past the front counter. I waved at Freddy, who was busy tossing a large pizza dough into the air.

"Use your back door Freddy?"

"What for?"

I pulled out my FBI shield and waved it at him.

"Help yourself."

Pushing the lock on the back door, I stepped into the alley. I figured if he was still on the job, he would park somewhere to watch my car. That meant he would most likely be behind the car; I turned right. I crossed the street at the end of the alley and walked another block before going back to Belmont and turning toward the pizza parlor.

In half a block, I spotted the Mercedes sitting in a no parking zone, next to a fire hydrant. As inconspicuously as I could, I eased up behind the car. The driver was using his hand to shield his eyes from the last bright rays of the sun and leaning forward over the steering wheel. His attention focused ahead.

I drew my Glock and eased along the driver's side. Raising the gun, I tapped on the driver-side window with the barrel—politely. He almost broke his neck, his head turned so fast, his eyes the size of dinner plates. I wiggled the barrel of the Glock, motioning him to roll down the window. He fumbled with it for several seconds before getting it to wind down.

I was immediately assaulted by the odor of stale fast food and sweat. Empty food wrappers littered the passenger seat and floor. The back seat was filled with wadded and wrinkled clothes.

"Y-y-yes sir?"

"Put your hands on the steering wheel where I can see them."

"Yes sir."

"Explain."

"Um…explain?"

"Why are you following me?"

"You…you're Thomas Quinn."

"Not a mystery."

"I'm supposed to meet you."

"There are better ways to do that."

"I wanted to meet you at the FBI office but you haven't been there for weeks."

"It's been two weeks."

"That's how long I've been looking for you."

I was still standing in the busy street, and I hadn't put my pistol back in its holster. If someone wanted to call the police, they would have been justified. I looked at him. He didn't look like a guy down on his luck. He had a few days of razor stubble, but his haircut was current. He was wearing an Oxford shirt with a faint pinstripe. His cellphone was plugged into the auxiliary and sitting in a holder on the console. He looked like a guy whose wife had thrown him out of their comfortable suburban home and all their friends were only her friends now.

"Why do you want to get in touch with me?"

"That's what he told me to do. He said you'd do for me."

"Who told you? What's your name?"

"I'm J.J...J.J. Rathcoate. Harry told me to contact you. He said you'd protect me. I tried to go to the police but they just laughed when I told them I was getting threats. Then you weren't at the bureau. There were cars parked across the street from my house every day and strange hang-up calls."

Now that he was talking, it was all coming out at once.

"My secretary got stopped on her way to lunch and her purse was searched by cops. It scared her so bad she threatened to quit. I stopped going home after work, then this week I just stopped going to work altogether. Yesterday, I spotted you and decided to stay as close as possible until you went back to work. I need protection. They're after me."

I put my gun away.

"You were Harry's attorney."

"Yes."

"Who's they? Who's after you?"

"I don't know."

"Do you know what they want? Whoever they are."

"No, not really. I mean, I did all of Harry's last business arrangements. I distributed the letters and cashier's checks. I've done nothing else, and mostly, the business that Harry was doing is now complete."

I looked around. Cars were passing us slowly, giving me dirty looks for delaying them from whatever they were rushing to. The evening light was settling into the neighborhood and the heat of the day was dissolving into a cool humidity. The volume of traffic hinted that there was a game tonight at Wrigley Field. I made a quick decision.

"Follow me once I get back to my car. Don't lose me."

Back in my car, I headed east until I turned on Elston and headed south into the city. I wanted to avoid as much traffic, or eyes, as I could. True to his instructions, J. J. Rathcoate was following me so closely he was going to leave an impression of my license plate on his front bumper. At Milwaukee Avenue, I headed into the loop and at the river, I pulled into the parking garage of the Sheraton Hotel and parked as far from the elevators as I could. J.J. was right behind me.

We walked to the elevators, J. J. Rathcoate wrestling an armload of wrinkled smelly laundry and me with my head on a swivel. In the elevator, I gave him my most serious look.

"Leave all that shit in the elevator. Check in at the front desk, two keys, don't talk, don't be nice, just business. Put the room on a card you don't usually use, and book it for a week. We can always check out early if we need to."

"That's going to be expensive!"

"Dying isn't any cheaper. I'll hold the elevator."

He nodded, then bent down and gently lowered his only possessions into the elevator's corner. When the doors opened in the lobby he checked his wallet, nodded to me again and walked out. It was Sunday night, business travelers with an eye to their bottom line generally didn't check in until Monday. Weekend trysts and get-a-ways had checked out before noon; the lobby was quiet. I stepped into the open doorway of the elevator and watched him. No one new came into or left the lobby in the three minutes it took to check him in. As far as I could tell he was unnoticed and undetected. I wondered if all this might be the result of an overactive imagination and if none of it was real. But it was his dime so I took it as seriously as I should.

Once Rathcoate was back in the elevator, he immediately retrieved his laundry and huddled in the corner away from me. I took the room keys from him when we reached the floor, left him in the elevator and checked the hallway. I wanted him to know that I was taking his paranoia seriously, so I made sure I was thorough. They had given him a corner room at the end of the hall, which was fitting for a week-long booking. A nice room with a view looking out across the Chicago river and the brightly illuminated Wrigley Building in the evening light. I closed the drapes and retrieved him from the elevator.

"Okay Mr. Rathcoate, you should be pretty safe here for now. If someone is looking for you, it would be hard to imagine they would find you here. I'm going to stay with you tonight, but tomorrow I'll go to the bureau and see about getting you into some sort of protection detail."

"Aren't you going to take me with you?"

"No."

Rathcoate's eyes widened and he looked like he was going to break down in tears. I recognized that we hadn't spoken more than a few sentences since we first met.

"Look," I sat down on the edge of the bed, "this is all a lot. There's not a lot of evidence to support your fears besides what you've observed yourself. I understand the impact that Harry Beech had on your life, Lord knows, I've been looking over my shoulder for weeks now and I know absolutely nothing about Harry's business or his dealings. So I get it. You probably should be a little concerned because you probably know things that other people might want to know."

"That's just it; I don't know anything about what Harry did. I knew who he was yeah, but he didn't share anything else. He would give me an assignment, a task or he would need something legal executed and I'd do it but that was it. We rarely talked. Most of what we did was through the mail. What Harry really needed was an accountant, he had so much business but it was just business. Monthly fees, payments, the widow's fund, stuff like that. Just money in and money out kind of stuff."

"Wait! what? What was the widow's fund?"

"That was one of Harry's accounts."

"What was it for?"

"I don't know. It was just one of the things that came up regularly. You know, like quarterly. Just another bill. That's why he needed an accountant, not an attorney really."

"Okay, that's for later. Now we've got to get it together for tomorrow. Give me your car keys."

"What for?"

"I don't want your car anywhere near where you are. If they find it in the parking garage, they'll find you in the hotel soon enough. I need to move it somewhere else."

"I need my car."

"It won't do you any good right now, and you can always get it when the time comes."

"But…"

"I'll make sure it's safe. You've gotta trust me on this now."

"But…I need my car."

"I'm going to put it in a safe place so nobody messes with it. It'll be there for you when the time comes. For now, we got to make sure that you're as safe as we can make you. That car is like a beacon saying, 'Come and get me.' So we'll put it someplace else for now. Okay?"

"I don't like it."

"You asked for my help. This is one of the things that I think you should do. If you want our help, you will have to do what we say for a little while. Once this blows over you can go back to your old life, but for right now you should take my advice."

Trouble

The little Benz was fun to drive, even if it was only going to be for a few blocks. I drove south and picked one of the parking garages on Wabash. Parking on the upper level, I backed into the space and gave the interior a good 'once over.' The car was new, with less than two thousand miles on the odometer. The glove box revealed the usual instruction book on all the car's gadgets and a separate book just for the Bluetooth screen and everything it knew how to do. Underneath were the sales receipt and sales documentation for the car. It had been purchased, apparently with cash or a check, exactly two weeks and one day ago.

Well, well J. J., that must have been one heck of a retainer fee, I thought.

The rest of the inside of the car didn't have enough time to accumulate the detritus of the life we spend in our cars. Except for a lingering stale laundry aroma and new leather, there was nothing to find. The trunk was next and things became immediately a lot more interesting.

There were two cartons, big ones. The type of file box that a corporate business used to store important but stale documentation. Both boxes were full. The first file I pulled out was labeled Agribank and filled with ledger entries and official statements of accounts on file. The second file was labeled Citibank and had similar ledgers. It also contained what appeared to be a safe deposit box key. I pulled one at random, Hang Seng Bank, Hong Kong. Each file was not new, and appeared to contain what was probably years of entries. I whistled; there was a lot of money being managed, from what I could see with a cursory look. At the back of the box there were several file folders containing hand-written correspondence and two computer flash drives.

I dropped the two flash drives into my pocket and set aside the correspondence for some later light reading. I lifted the lid on the other box. Whereas the first box had been confusing, the second box literally took my breath away. There was nothing to examine; there was no mystery to the contents. The second box was filled with money. There were strapped bundles of hundreds and bricks of ten strapped bundles each. There were a few bundles of fifties and twenties. In a neat stack at the front of the box were several one-ounce gold bars. I put the lid back on the box and shut the trunk lid. For the second time in the last thirty minutes, I reassessed Mr. J. J. Rathcoate. Was he trying to get away with all this trunkful of trouble, or was he honestly trying to be a good citizen? Either way, he was in way more trouble than I had been giving him credit for. The second box alone contained at least half-a-million dollars in untraceable cash. There were plenty of people, even in my neighborhood, who would happily kill someone for that kind of money.

I hiked back to the Sheraton and picked up my car. There was no sense in checking on Rathcoate; I had only been gone for an hour. Back in the parking garage on Wabash, I loaded the two cartons into the trunk of my car and paid the minimum parking fee to get back out on the street.

I turned north and headed back home. This time, I was far more paranoid and made several detours with my eyes glued to the rearview mirror. No headlights turned to follow that I could tell, but that was only half a comfort. Plenty of people already knew where I lived and how to find me. I was just trying to avoid any new ones.

I pulled up to the pizza parlor and lifted the money box off the back seat. Instead of going into the apartment entry, I wedged my way through the glass front door and straight back into the kitchen.

"Freddy, need a favor."

"What favor?"

"I need to put these in cold storage right away."

"What'ya got in there?"

"Nunya"

"What's nunya?"

"Nunya business, capiche?"

"Okay, okay put it in the walk-in freezer in the back."

"Mustn't touch."

"Don't worry, I got real problems. I don't need any of

yours. Just don't leave it here too long."

"One day, two max."

"Don't tell me nothin.' Just get it gone."

"Thanks Freddie." But then I had a second thought. "Hey Freddie?"

"Yeah."

"I need to borrow a car."

"What the fuck! I'm not in the Rent-A-Car business."

I took a band of fifties out of my pocket and broke the strap. I peeled off five bills and handed it to him.

"I need a different car."

"Shit man! This is a lot of bread." He counted them again. "Okay…yeah take my ride." He fished his keys out of his pocket. "The Toyota pickup parked down around the corner. It's red, don't fuck it up. I love that truck."

I gave him my keys and told him to park it somewhere else when he got the chance.

Back on the street in an old Toyota pickup truck, I maneuvered the traffic back to the Sheraton and parked near the elevator. I went to the bar in the lobby and ordered a double shot of Jack Daniels and a beer chaser. I looked at the guy in the mirror behind the bar. I thought about how this was not what I thought working for the FBI would be like. My Army career had not been heroic; it had been tragic. I had imagined my law enforcement career with historic arrests and nationally televised criminal investigations and with me at the center of the action. I had not imagined daily tests of my personal sense of integrity or my understanding of right and wrong as a black and white consideration. In the span of a few months all of those things, the imaginary and the real, had spun themselves into a confusing kaleidoscope of dark and light. The imagined danger of FBI law enforcement had been replaced with a cold reality where people suffered consequences and I might be next. I signaled the bartender for a second round, toasted myself in the mirror, left a twenty-dollar tip and headed for the elevator and Mr. J. J. Rathcoate.

U.S. Marshals

I was standing at the chief's desk with a file box in my hands when he walked in with his coffee in one hand. He gave me a half smile and hung up his jacket before sitting down, lighting a cigarette and leaning back in his chair.

"Welcome back! Ready to join the useless rabble?"

"Chief, I got a problem."

Ten minutes later.

"Well shit. I thought today was just gonna be just another fucking Monday." He waved one of the files over his head and pulled another out of the box with his free hand.

"Sorry Chief."

"Oh no, don't apologize. Things just got really interesting around here. You're right this guy is solid gold.

We got to protect him no matter how much he knows. Shit if he knows just jack shit about what kind of connection Harry Beech had, he's a real firecracker. We'll need to get the U.S. Marshalls on this. They do that stuff, not us. I'll do that first. Shit, we'll have to contact the Organized Crime Task Force too. God dammit, this is going to be more fun than I've had in a month."

Within an hour the office was filled with personnel. Besides myself, agent Bob English had joined us. Two U.S. Marshalls and the liaison officer from the Chicago Police Department stood along the wall.

"First things first. We don't have a lot of planning time. Once we have the guy, we can lock it down, but for now we'll just take this as professionally as possible."

Everyone nodded.

"How do we know he's still gonna be there?" The P.D. Liason asked.

"I made him promise." I answered. "He's scared as hell. He's not going to leave his only lifeline. Besides, I took his keys and moved his car so he couldn't find it."

I dropped the key set on the desk.

"Okay, the Marshalls will go directly to the room. They'll take him into custody and escort him through the lobby. Assistance will be provided by the Chicago P.D. Agent English and Agent Quinn will assist and take possession of his vehicle and other possessions. The Marshalls will be charged with providing a safe house, location to be determined.

"Other than that we should be just doing a routine arrest. Any questions?"

I handed the room key to the Marshal on my left. He nodded to me and waved me through ahead of him when the door opened. We were all immediately hit with the icy cold blast of too much air conditioning and a fetid smell. The marshal pushed past me his gun drawn, his partner right behind him. I didn't understand but followed.

Around the corner J.J. Rathcoate greeted us with an insane grin from where he was sitting. He was seated in a chair, naked and zip-tied to it. The chair sat in the middle of an 8X8 plastic tarp that had captured almost all of his blood loss. His body was covered with an uncountable number of slashes and sliced skin. His tongue had been removed. He had bled out slowly. He was still silently screaming in death.

"How can this be possible!? I was here just a few hours ago!" I was aghast.

Bob English leaned over and touched the body.

"Body temperature is almost normal. Ain't been dead long."

"I think you better back up a little and get your story straight Tom." The chief in his blue FBI jacket took in the scene in one sweep.

"I told you. I left here this morning. Rathcoate was nervous but okay. That was about seven. He was okay when I left. I've only been gone a few hours." I consulted my watch. "It's only just eleven now."

"How'd they know he was here." He got right in my face; his frown went all the way to his hairline. "And who the hell are they?"

"I don't know and I don't know."

"Okay, let's see if they left anything for us to find. Pretty goddammed unlikely. Shit, we have stepped on our dick's here. Shit!"

"I thought I covered my tracks Chief. I tried to follow protocol right down to the letter."

"That's a matter for a later discussion Tom. Does this guy have any personal effects?"

We spread out through the suite. The rooms had been tossed professionally. Everything had been moved but carefully put back to where it came from. There was nothing to find. Rathcoate's laundry had come back and had been hung in the bedroom closet.

"How did the laundry get in the closet?"

"Room service? I told him not to call room service or order anything. Goddammit I told him not to answer the door."

"Well he did."

"Where's his keys?" The tall Marshall asked. "We need to impound the car at the very least."

"Wabash Street parking garage. It's on the fourth level near the back."

The Chief was becoming despondent thinking about the paperwork. "Get that guy up here from the P.D., we're gonna need crime scene people in here. And a coroner, a friendly one."

Then he turned to me,

"Right now I've got no choice Tom. This was a person in your custody and now he's dead. You probably should have just taken him into custody, but I understand. I'm sorry Tom, as of right now you're on administrative leave. No questions; it's mandatory protocol. Give me your shield and gun; we'll be in touch."

The Widow's Fund

I had lied to the bureau chief and I suspected that he knew it. I wasn't even sure why I had. I had not done things according to the letter. I had moved the Rathcoate car. My fingerprints and DNA were probably all over the damn thing. I had taken possession of valuable evidence and turned some of it over to the authorities, but not all of it. Now I stood in the hotel lobby and watched the rush of police forensic teams, the ambulance and coroner's employees as they boarded the elevator. With every new arrival the gravity of my situation became increasingly evident. I felt bad about Rathcoate; he seemed an innocent participant and I said so when I gave my statement to the detective. No one ever deserved to die the way he had. It was a vision that would never leave my nightmares. And somehow through it all, I had managed to make my own situation even worse.

I stopped at the pizza place to pick up the remaining carton that I had left in the walk-in freezer. Then I dropped the truck keys on the counter and retrieved my car. Back downtown I pulled into the parking garage at the Sheraton again and drove to the top floor. Mindful of the security cameras in the parking garage I only removed the front license plates of the two cars parked nose in. It didn't matter that they didn't match, nobody ever checked to see if the front and back license plates matched on any car. Right now, I needed a new identity, so I got a new set of unmatched plates. It wasn't much of a disguise, but I decided to err on the side of caution and cover my ass as much as I could. Mine was not a notable car, it looked like a lot of the other ones on the street, so the license plate was probably the only way to identify it from the others. But I also knew that if they wanted to find me, the different plates would only buy me a few blocks head start.

I got on the Eisenhower and headed out of town, not stopping until I was forty miles out and the expressway disappeared into the Illinois toll road system out in the western suburbs. In Naperville I found a local hotel near the river with indoor parking. I emptied out the contents of the box onto the bed. The money was the easy part, four hundred and seventy thousand, eight hundred and forty dollars in cash. I had no way of calculating the value of the gold bullion.

I looked at the computer flash drives knowing full well that I should have turned them over too, along with the money. I couldn't even reason with myself why I had not. Neither of them had any label of identification. Then

I juggled the two safety deposit box keys in my hand; there were thousands of possibilities for where those keys would work, but they had been in the Citibank file so that would be a good start. All work that the FBI would probably be good at, but instead I had kept them. I dropped the keys in my other pocket.

Instead of grappling with my unexplainable career suicide, I went shopping. I didn't splurge, but I bought a seriously nice laptop computer and a good color printer at the computer big box store at the mall. I had them install a few extra programs that could read documents, PDF's and ledgers, not really knowing what might be on the flash drives from the box and headed back to the room.

The new computer was lightning fast and within moments a huge Excel ledger program launched. There were separate accounts for different banks, banks from all over the world. The first one, Agribank. There appeared to have been continuous deposits in varying amounts into an account that spanned decades. Withdrawals had been few and the account balance was considerable. There were regular transfers to other banks. I pulled up the Citibank file next, the story was the same. Anonymous deposits of varying amounts and occasional withdrawals. Again it appeared that the balance was in the millions of dollars.

I scrolled my way down the list of file folders. Almost at the bottom I struck the one I'd been hoping was there, labeled, 'Widow's Fund.'

Inside the file was a general ledger of accounts. A balance of deposits that were transfers from the other banks almost entirely, and the regular disbursement of these funds. It appeared that this was the account where most of the other bank transfers ended up because the balance was over a hundred million dollars. This account also listed disbursements; each disbursement was labeled and accounted for. Some were minor, only several thousand dollars at a time. These each had a name attached to them. Many of the names were widows corresponding to the file boxes on my desk back at the FBI. I had studied those files. They were here, widows, widowers in some cases, but I recognized the names, there they were along with dozens of others.

They were organized in a subfile; I flipped through the various pages, and they were listed in alphabetical order. Carol Abbott was the first page. She didn't have a file on my desk, but her husband did. Carol Abbott former wife of Kerry Abbott. Kerry Abbott gunned down outside of a restaurant on the south side of Chicago. The disbursements were in increments of ten thousand dollars every fiscal quarter for over twenty years, over eight hundred thousand dollars altogether. Six or seven pages further back, Jack DeRoos, former husband of Mabel DeRoos. Mabel DeRoos was another file on my desk, shot three times, twice in the head and once in the chest, left on a park bench on the Chicago lakefront. Disbursement one time only; seventy-five thousand dollars. Further back Rebecca Mencorini, quarterly payments. The third person in the file, filed under the 'C's', Sally Carlisle, quarterly disbursements for the last twelve years.

I understood about Sally, I knew the story. Tim Carlisle had been burned alive in what was assumed to be a minor traffic accident, but under suspicious circumstances. Bobby Dey-Dey had corroborated the crime when I had asked him about it. He was probably responsible for the fire, but we would never know now.

I pushed my chair back and considered. I didn't know how long my administrative leave could be, but I guessed it would be over two weeks, likely at least a month. That gave me a month to figure out a mystery that made no sense at all. Where was all the money coming from? The amounts of money going to the widows and other crime victims was minuscule compared to the amounts coming in regularly. What was more, there were deposits that had occurred since Harry's death; his dying had not stopped the flow of money into the accounts, or the various transfers and disbursements that had been happening despite his incarceration, at least so far.

Somewhere, somehow there had to be something or someone that controlled everything. Money was moving from one account to another, and most, if not all of them, were offshore. There was no way to estimate how much there was in any given place at any given time. It was a lot of balls to keep juggling in the air at one time, and whoever they were—they seemed to be good at what they did.

I had little doubt that it was the box filled with files and not the box of money that had gotten J.J. Rathcoate killed. I printed and spread out the sheets from the Widow's Fund file across the bed. The oldest entries dated back almost forty years, and featured names that I recognized from the television news. There were other names that I didn't recognize, a progression of members of a secret club with only one requirement for membership. Someone they loved had to be dead, not just dead, but it appeared that they had to be dead by another's hand. Of the names I recognized, every one of them had met an untimely death through criminal violence.

The trend repeated itself page after page. There would be a new name added periodically and likewise a periodic entry that ended someone's membership. These were entered with the simple explanation—deceased. Apparently the benefit continued from inception until the beneficiary had passed away.

There were dozens of names that had gone under the radar with the FBI and local police as far as the file box on my desk was concerned, but those names too were in the Widow's Fund file. There was a much deeper story behind every one of those names than I had given them credit for.

J. J. Rathcoate had died because of this file.

I started doing the math. I was the last person to see Rathcoate alive. My DNA and fingerprints were all over the inside of his car, which had disappeared from the scene of the crime. When I had the chance to tell my supervisor and come clean, I had not. I had reacted by instinct instead of as an officer of the law, and now I was going to have a hard time finding my way back. I was withholding evidence that spoke to a much larger crime. I had been placed on leave so I couldn't continue any real form of an investigation even if I could imagine where the next step in that investigation needed to go—which I couldn't. Somehow, accidentally, I had succeeded in creating myself as the perfect patsy for a murder that had taken place in a busy Chicago hotel and probably had produced little or no forensic evidence. A crime like that had political implications and would need solving quickly. If the roles were reversed I would have a hard time believing my story of innocence. If I hadn't been up until now, I decided that it was time to get seriously paranoid.

For a moment, I didn't think it could possibly get worse, until I pulled out the first flash drive and put in the second. How much worse it could get became immediately apparent. Contained in the second drive were a multitude of files, all listed in alphabetical order. The first file labeled, 'Contacts', was a listing of all of the banks that had accounts in the first drive and their personal human contacts. The file labeled 'Password', caught my eye and I clicked on it. There followed a small ledger, listing each individual bank, and the account password to access that account. Sweat started to break out on my forehead. Then I noticed that the next one below 'Contacts' was labeled 'Council.' I got up and paced the room, then I hit the mini-bar. The two little whiskeys weren't enough, I looked at the vodka and shook my head. I called room service.

"I'm planning on having a few people in. Will you please send up a fifth of Jack Daniels whiskey and a bucket of ice?"

"Do you need extra glasses sir?"

"Glasses? Um, yes sure, a couple extra glasses." There was no sense letting him know I'd be drinking alone.

"Right away sir. It will be there shortly. Will there be anything else?"

"No that's all. Thank you."

I was still pacing back and forth staring at the computer screen when the knock came at the door. Looking through the fisheye peephole showed a young Hispanic kid with his face about three inches away from the hole in the door and looking nervous. I unlocked the door and cautiously opened it. The kid stood there with an ice bucket and a bottle of Jack wrapped in a towel. Behind him stood Jerry Beech.

"I think your guest is here sir. Where would you like me to put this?"

I looked at Jerry, he wasn't smiling and before I could respond he was joined by Greg. The two of them didn't leave a lot of extra room in the hallway.

"I'll take those," Jerry spoke and pushed past the young waiter taking the bottle and bucket with him. "We'll need another one of these in about thirty minutes."

I was paralyzed into inaction. Greg pushed past me and into the room. The two of them started opening the bottle and putting ice in glasses. I started to close the door without taking my eyes off of them, but the door resisted. Then it pushed back and I opened it again. Sally Carlisle stood there looking expectant.

"Aren't you going to tip him?"

I fumbled out another twenty and gave the server a shaky smile. He looked like the ghost of his grandmother had just said 'howdy.'

"Please. We need a few more chairs, and bring a bottle of vodka, not just vodka, good vodka and one of dry vermouth along with that second bottle of Jack Daniels please." Sally, as usual, had taken charge. "Oh, and some nice olives too please."

She nodded at me and signaled with her chin. I gave the kid another twenty.

Once the door was closed I stood there unable to move. Jerry had taken a seat on the edge of the bed and Greg was sitting on the window sill; both looking at me with their arms crossed. Sally sat down in the office chair and punched a button on the computer. When the screen

came up she looked at it for a moment.
"Oh my! Somebody's in way over their head."

A Bedtime Story

My knees buckled while visions of J. J. Rathcoate played across my memories.

"How did you know where I was?"

"Well Tom," she rolled back in the chair and crossed her arms, "we've had a tracker on your car ever since the day of the funeral. We weren't the only ones that wanted to know what you were up to, but we wanted to be the first ones to know. You really had me worried when the car didn't move yesterday, that was very clever. It was just lucky for us that the tracker on Mr. Rathcoate moved when you moved for a while yesterday."

"You put a tracker on my car?"

"Yes. I was worried about you."

I shrugged that off, "How did you know about

Rathcoate?"

We were interrupted by the young staffer bringing in extra chairs. He was followed by a cart with the drinks. As soon as they left, Sally twisted in her chair, "Boys go down to the front desk." Sally spoke to Greg and Jerry, "Book rooms on each side of us and both of them across the hallway. If they're already rented get them to relocate those people. Make it worth their while."

Greg and Jerry left and Sally lounged back in the office chair. a tumbler of martini on the rocks in her hand.

"I didn't know about Rathcoate until you mentioned his name. The letter that you brought me was from Harry not him. The check Harry sent was a joke. An old bet that we'd made years ago. Who would die first. It was a certified check for twenty-five cents. I wanted to know if he knew anything more about Harry's affairs so I went to see Rathcoate. He was completely full of himself and unfortunately, he was not completely forthright. I know what that looks like when I see it. I decided to see what he was really up to. Apparently dying if I'm not mistaken."

"Do you know anything about his killing Sally?"

"It was on the five o'clock news." She sipped her drink.

I was still standing by the door. Sally waved a hand at the computer.

"What do you have there Tom?"

"It was on the thumb drive that Rathcoate gave me."

"He gave you!?"

"Well, I relieved him of them."

"Did he give you anything else?"

"I turned in a file box of banking ledgers."

"Interesting."

She took a long drink while she met my eyes over the rim of her glass while she raised one eyebrow.

"There was a box of cash, a couple safety deposit keys, and these flash drives."

She showed a cheshire smile, "You've been busy. Learn anything?"

"Why are you here—Sally?"

She was too coy, too cool. She sat there jiggling the ice in her now empty glass with a half-smile. I had run out of new places to sweat out of. Jerry and Greg would be back any minute.

"Why Tom please sit down. Get comfortable. I'm here to tell you a story."

"I don't think I can get comfortable. To be honest, I'm a long way from comfortable Sally. What happens when Greg and Jerry get back?"

"Oh relax Tom. They've heard the story before."

That did nothing to help me relax. Neither did the arrival of the two goliath brothers. They immediately poured glasses and found seats with almost zero emotion. I poured four fingers of whiskey in a glass and sat in the most distant chair, the one closest to the door. I drained my glass and poured another one. I looked at the three of them lounging in their most uncomfortable chairs. They were relaxed, it didn't appear, at least for now, that they intended me any harm.

"Alright Tom. You have all the pieces; you just don't know it yet. I'm going to try and put the puzzle together for you. Unfortunately for you, it probably won't do you a bit of good."

"What does that mean Sally?"

"Listen to the story first Tom, then you decide. All

right?"

I raised my eyebrows and took a drink.

"What if I told you that what you know about Harry's crime is wrong? Would you believe me?"

"The evidence strongly supports Harry's conviction Sally."

"What if there was an eye witness that could dispute the facts? Would you believe it?"

"I'd want to know why the person never stepped forward at the trial."

"Let me tell you the real story Tom. Randa Simonsen was just another street rat that Harry somehow saw something special in. He wasn't wrong either. If you told her how to do something, she couldn't do it but if you showed her, she could do it immediately. Every lesson that Harry taught her she mastered. Every trick, every turn of the tongue, she got it immediately.

"Harry brought her to me to teach manners and fashion. It was the same. It was like watching a flower bloom in front of you. The clothes, the makeup, the walk it was like she was born to it. Your dad, Mickey taught her locks and doors. In no time she could open, doors, windows and small safes."

"Wait! My dad? My dad taught her?"

"You're dad was a great guy. He adored Randa. We all did, but none of us more than Harry. He was twenty years older than she was, but you could tell that she was the only one that had ever turned his head.

"Randa was oblivious. She tackled every assignment he gave her, until that one night. That night tilted the table, and she got a taste for it. There was no doubt that she was good at it, but pretty soon it was all that she wanted to do. No more pillow talk confessions with politicians, no more arm-candy escort work; only the wet work. She was addicted and as a result in high demand.

"Then along came dipshit Dugan."

"I know that part of the story."

"Well it didn't take long for that beautiful relationship to go south. Dugan was useless, and Randa got bored. She tried, really she tried. When one kid wasn't enough, she had another baby. Even with two kids, she wanted more. She and Harry, heck all of us, had remained close, she asked for her job back and he said no."

"You told me you didn't know anything about that."

"A white lie. I'm entitled. Harry couldn't be swayed, he wanted Randa to be his little dream. The house in the suburbs, a couple kids, PTA meetings. That was Harry's idea of paradise. He wanted that for Randa, but she didn't. She took a side job.

"It might have been that she was just out of practice, or that she underestimated the target. Either way, it went badly wrong. Badly. It made the headlines, the national headlines. It was a mess. The client wasn't satisfied and the friends of the victim were equally unhappy. Someone who is a freelancer in that field has a very short life expectancy. Without an umbrella to operate under they lack any protection."

"Protection from who?"

Sally rolled her chair forward and tapped the computer to refresh the screen. When it opened, she waved her hand at the screen and gave me a knowing look.

"Almost immediately there were multiple factions that were engaged in trying to locate the new freelancer.

Randa knew that they would figure it out and went to Harry to ask for his help; and his forgiveness. There was almost nothing that Randa would have been able to do that would have alienated Harry, but his options to help her were limited. If a contract had been let, he couldn't stop its execution. The only way to protect her was to make her his own. By his very reputation, no one would fuck with what was Harry's. Harry proposed matrimony, Randa accepted."

"So he didn't shoot her?"

"Don't get ahead of yourself Tom."

"On the day that they were to be married we drove to Randa's to pick her up and take her with us to the courthouse. After all, Harry had never been married, I was excited to go along. The fact I also loved Randa helped too. It was supposed to be a joyous occasion."

Sally drained her glass, and poured another one on the old ice. She didn't even bother to wave the bottle of vermouth at it. In one swallow she drained that one too.

"We heard the shots as we pulled into the driveway. I'll never forget it. Pop, pop, pop…pop." She sucked the ice out of her glass. "Harry was out of the car like a shot. I was right behind him. At the door we met Tom Janes who took a swing at Harry. He missed Harry and hit me in the shoulder and knocked me down. A second man came rushing forward and aimed at Harry with a pistol. Harry grabbed the barrel and they wrestled for the gun. I tried to get up but Janes punched me in the face and knocked me down again.

"Harry got the gun, and turned it around. He shot Janes in the face, the tall skinny guy pushed out the door and ran off the porch. Harry aimed and pulled the trigger multiple times, but only one shot fired. I would swear on a stack of bibles that he hit him, but then I was pretty woozy.

"Pretty soon Harry came back out of the house still holding the gun. He got me back on my feet and told me to vamoose. He told me to get the hell out of there. I wanted him to go with me, but he wouldn't. He said he couldn't. He said he couldn't because then there would be no justice."

Sally sighed deeply, then poured another drink and sipped it, "I think Harry died that day. It just took a while for his body to get the message."

"Shit."

"So?"

"So the sixth bullet is in somebody's ass?"

"Yes, I think so."

The Sixth Bullet

"Do you have any idea who's ass?"

"No. I didn't get a good look at him. My vision was blurred. I had a cut above my eye," she pulled her hair back and showed me a narrow white scar that disappeared into her right eyebrow, "and I was lying on the porch. I got a close-up look at Janes. He was lying right next to me but all I saw of the other guy was that he looked tall and was wearing plain Oxford dress shoes."

"Where did this guy go?"

"I don't know. He ran around the house and away through the back yard. There wasn't any car parked on the street in front of the house that I remember."

I looked out the window, past Greg sitting on the sill. The narrative tracked, I could imagine the entire scene and how it fit with the crime scene photos that I had studied. It was believable, but I also reasoned that Sally had twelve years to practice the story and it could be just a fabrication. In either case she was correct, there was nothing I could do about it. Harry was gone, Randa Dugan was gone, Tom Janes also gone. Somehow, even the fact that my father, Mickey Frances was gone just made it seem more final. The chessboard was cleared, only the queen remained, only Sally was left.

"You're right; there's nothing that anyone of us can do about it anymore."

"I thought so too for a long time, but now I'm thinking differently."

"What?"

"My brother Andy, died the same way that Randa did." She nodded at Jerry, "These guys father, Andrew. Shot three times in the back and once more in the chest. We think that whoever killed Randa was really there for Harry. We just arrived a little early because we were excited. Whoever got Andy, wanted Harry too. Randa was just a bonus."

"That is kind of a stretch to get with that reasoning Sally."

Sally rolled back from the desk and waved her hand at the computer.

"Go ahead and check. These boys were still underage minors. Check the file and see if there's a Widow's Fund entry for Andy. There isn't one and do you know why? It wasn't an accident or a random altercation. It was a hit, and it wasn't sanctioned."

"What do you mean sanctioned?"

"Boys. I think there's someone that Tom needs to

meet don't you?"

"What do you mean?" I had no gun anymore, and I was sure I was no match for both Greg and Jerry.

"There's someone you need to meet. I had the thought that our conversation might go this way, so I've already spoken to him and he is expecting you."

Then she saw my tense mood, and relaxed.

"Relax Tom, pack up all of this stuff and bring it with you. You're going to enjoy this. I promise."

Hidden

With that promise they rose as one. Jerry walked past me as I flinched and opened the door. With a gracious wave he directed me out into the hallway. Greg closed up the laptop, after handing me the two flash drives, he set it on top of the file box and headed out the door. I pocketed the two flash drives, wishing that I had left the box of money somewhere else.

True to form, the oversize SUV stood in the front parking slot reserved for loading and unloading. They directed me to sit in the front passenger seat. Jerry drove and Greg took the seat directly behind me. The inside of the car was overheated after sitting in the hot June sun but my ass cheeks had run out of sweat already.

"We are not going far Tom." Sally from the back seat

fumbled in her handbag and produced a cigarette. Rolling the window down, she lit it and took a nervous drag. "Take it away Jerry."

We continued west, first on the Interstate, then on a two-lane highway. After thirty minutes we turned onto a graveled country road. A few miles later we came upon a mailbox that stood at the end of a country lane that disappeared into a dense growth of trees. The mailbox hung on a drunken post with its door hanging open to the elements. There was no name or number on the box. We turned into the lane.

Once within the trees the lane dropped down into a steep gully. At the bottom, unseen from the road was a small cluster of stone buildings. A small ranch house, a barn and a tool shed. The surrounding lawn was immaculately trimmed and all the exposed wood showed fresh paint. It felt a million miles from civilization, walled in behind an impenetrable hedge.

Sitting in a wooden rocker on the front porch was an elderly man smoking a cigarette and rocking as he watched us pull up in front of him.

"Stay in the car." Sally stepped out and walked up to the porch. She shook his hand, then after a brief conversation she waved us out of the SUV. I was glad to have an excuse to not be sitting in front of Greg and stepped out. With another wave Sally signaled me to approach.

"Tom, this is the fellow that I wanted you to meet. I think you'll like what he might have to say."

"How you doing Tom?" The man rose to his feet. He wore a straw panama hat, a Hawaiian print shirt and fresh pressed khakis. On his feet were hirachi sandals, his toenails looked polished. He held out his hand to be shaken, I looked at Sally confused.

"Tom, I'd like you to meet Mr. Charlie Halliday. Charlie, this is my friend Tom Quinn."

It Was Harry

Just when you don't think anything can still surprise you.

"*The* Mr. Charlie Halliday?" I had never met a ghost before.

"The one and only. I bet you'd like to ask me a few questions wouldn't you?"

"Where do I start?"

"It's going to cool off once the sun starts to go down. Let's go sit on the patio out back. It feels like a margarita night to me. How about you Sal?"

"If you're cookin', I'm eating. Margaritas it is."

"That's how we start Tom. With drinks and a few brats on the grill."

Somehow I'd forgotten to eat all day. Dinner; beer brats and baked beans was substantial, and in spite of me, it was delicious too. Pitchers of margarita were passed around and I relaxed into a semi-euphoric state. As the evening light settled in Charlie lit a fire in the stone fireplace and the five of us sat in a semi-circle of warmth.

"It was Harry. He's the one that started it all."

"Started what?"

"The Consortium. What you've been studying. Where all the money is coming from."

"It's a consortium?"

"That loosely describes it yes, a loose alliance you could say. Sometimes willingly cooperative and sometimes reluctantly so. It was Harry's plan, way back then when we were still young and foolish."

"But…there's so much money. What's it from?"

"Okay," Charlie waved his glass in the air, "Imagine this." He took a long drink, "Imagine, lets say, Chicago as a big apple pie. It's too big to handle as one thing, so piece by piece we divide it up into pieces that can be managed individually. Inside the pie, there are pieces within pieces. For instance, there's the South Side, but inside that is prostitution, drugs, gambling and trafficking. Each one of those endeavors has to be managed, and those efforts have to be reported back to the main managers. Across the Urban Chicago area and the subsequent Suburban areas the pieces are divided up, and the sub-managers are assigned.

"There is tacit agreement that each group has

sovereignty in their own designated areas and they enter other areas at their own peril. It is an extremely competitive lifestyle and there is much jockeying for position. Some things are gained, some things are lost. Occasionally, something or someone becomes intolerable to one or the other faction. That something or someone has become a significant enough roadblock that it requires elimination, an unmanageable situation with no other apparent resolution. However adverse one party views this person or thing, there are other parties that still feel that it has value. The decision of elimination is discussed, negotiated, an agreement is reached, an amount is assessed, a tithe is paid. The thing or person is eliminated.

"By agreement, the arrived at amount includes compensation for the innocent individuals affected by the aforesaid agreement. Businesses are affected, family members for them there would be no other form of justice. Business decisions on a large scale that previously had no recourse, no hope of recovery from emotional disaster now had the; Widow's Fund. Now kids went to college, trade schools. Now widows could rise up and gain the status that money could buy. Now businesses could learn from their mistakes and streamline operation, become more efficient.

"Instead of continued squaller, neighborhoods thrived. Investment in communities rose, and small businesses were encouraged and funded. The Consortium was founded. Harry always spoke about the need for justice, not the winning or losing but the final justice of any situation. He wanted both sides of the coin, the win and the lose. In the end, they agreed and a council was formed. Their decisions were final and the accounts were created.

"The initial creation was a deposit of one million, six hundred and fifty thousand dollars that I personally provided to start the fund, compliments of the Teamsters Fund. That original deposit was with what is now J.P. Morgan-Chase, all of the other accounts have grown out of that since then. The fund invests in stocks, bonds and precious metals. The fund itself has grown to a modest amount, somewhere over three billion dollars as of the last quarterly reports. Several of our companies trade on the New York Stock Exchange."

"So? Do you manage all that from here?"

"Ha, that's a good one. Nope, I don't know jackshit about ledgers and balancing accounts and statements. I've got accountants to manage all that. Lots of them. We keep money moving. From one place to another, never in one place too long. Arriving at the Widow's Fund only in time for quarterly disbursements. At this point I suspect that the quarterly payments to the various factions has become a primary source of income for them."

"But why? Why are you doing all of this?"

"Why? Because otherwise there would be no justice."

"Justice? I understand what you're saying, but these are life and death decisions. People are dying, its barbaric in reality."

"Yes, it is."

"So where's the justice?"

"You have to step back from the emotional component Tom. Try and just consider it from a business standpoint. One company is doing business with their commodity. Another company, or individual is jealous, they want a share, they start pushing into someone else's territory.

What starts out as an annoyance, grows into animosity. Negotiations break down. Now business is compromised, trusted confederates start to question who might be in control tomorrow. Alliances begin to unravel. The resolution is to eliminate the virus, and get back to business.

"For those sticky decisions, in the old days before the consortium was formed one act triggered an equal and opposite reaction. The factions went to war over things like that. The two sides fought each other, both trying to get the last word. While that went on, both of their businesses suffered, there manpower was tied up in useless acts of retribution. Profits dropped and while they were distracted; they became vulnerable to other factions. There was constant strife. Someone was always trying to exact revenge.

"That's where Harry came in. Harry fixed things. He was already the person most people went to for the kind of arrangements we're discussing. Harry had an encyclopedic knowledge of people and their skill sets that he could call on for various services. One by one Harry spoke to first the South Side faction, the North Sider's, the inner-city gangs. Instead of the constant threat of war, Harry talked to them about a more civilized approach. He had a vision for moving to a different level of operation and growth toward legitimate status.

"Harry painted a picture of a seamless business model with each of the various groups allowed to operate as usual, but with the added benefit of a strong deterrent to encroachment. The model that Harry proposed also provided for incremental investment in a fund that would build into available cash for future investment, both in their own business ventures and joint mutual development. The dividends to be paid quarterly."

Charlie got up and put more wood on the fire, then he stepped in front of me and pushed his hat back on his head.

"I was skeptical. The Teamster's and their fund was a lost cause. Jimmy Hoffa was going to get what he deserved, but the money was already gone. The accountants that I had were heartbroken to see the fund depleted, we had all imagined different uses for the money. I took Harry to meet with them and see if his plan had any merit. They were unanimous in their agreement. It was a good plan if the factions would agree to it. I got on board then."

"How did you get them all to agree?"

"That actually ended up being the easy part. Harry engineered it. He called for a council meeting of sorts held at a neutral location. Harry's reputation was good enough so that they all agreed to hear him out."

"Did they agree?"

"No, quite the opposite. The meeting took all day. There was shouting, swearing and a couple of fist fights broke out, but Harry kept bringing them back to the discussion. I thought we would get them more in agreement when I confessed that I had a million and a half to start the initial investment. That didn't do it either. They simply wouldn't believe they were not sacrificing any of their own autonomy. They didn't see the golden opportunity. No one at the table trusted anyone else at the table."

"So, how did it get where it is today?"

"Harry of course. Harry was a very smart cookie, but

he had gotten where he was with hard knuckles. Harry was a hard ass underneath it all."

"Believe me, he was the toughest guy I ever met."

"Harry told them that there was no one at the conference table who was safe. Essentially, that Baba Yaga could come for any one of them at any time. He said it didn't matter how high up the ladder they were. But he said that this consortium he proposed would put an end to that fear. The consortium would provide a buffer, and a place for negotiation."

"Did it work?"

"Nope."

"Nope?"

"They all thought they were too big to be touched. They didn't think anyone could reach that high."

"So it was dead in the water."

"The meeting was about to break up when Andy Beech came into the room with a stack of the afternoon papers under his arm. He passed them out to all the members, the headline was stark, 'Hoffa disappears.' Everyone went home. Two days later, the meeting reconvened. This time there were more heads nodding than heads shaking. Hoffa had vanished without a trace in Detroit. In most people's opinion Hoffa had seemed completely untouchable, his disappearance was too much of a coincidence for anyone to believe that Harry had not had something to do with it. The Consortium was formed. The investments began. Since that time, there has not been a gangland war in Chicago or anywhere else with Chicago's influence."

There's A Rat

"But now there's a rat in the wood pile."

"Not just now, but for a while. It started before Randa Dugan, just a nibble here or a brush-by there, but yes someone has been quietly trying to work their way around our safeguards. Trying to block our efforts to move forward. The unsanctioned acts are a worry for everyone in the Consortium. None of us want to go back to the old days."

"Beside those of Andy Beech and Randa Dugan were there others?"

"At least one a year. Every investigation, both ours and the police, have hit dead-ends. We can't figure out where they get their intelligence to pick their victims, but all the victims have one thing in common. They all were instrumental in developing and maintaining the fund and the Consortium."

"But why? If there's been relative peace its beneficial for everyone on both sides of the law."

"Consider this then. What if the take down at Randa's had exactly the desired effect intended. What if taking out Harry wasn't enough for them? What if they wanted to destroy him completely? There was only one way to do that."

"You mean through Miranda Dugan?"

"Yes, exactly. She was the one thing he valued over all else. By killing her and the children, everything that mattered to Harry was snuffed out. Then setting him up to take the fall for it was the final death blow. He lost the will to fight instantly and we've spent the last twelve years trying to figure it out."

"What did you find out? Anything I can use?"

"We think Andy was getting close. He got quiet right at the end and was spending a lot of time downtown going through newspaper archives. He never said why, but then they took him out too."

"Shit. Is it coming from the outside or the inside? Could it be somebody like Joe Battaglia?"

"Joe's name is high on the list." Sally waved her glass at the fire. "He's got an ax to grind, his stepson was a sanctioned job. Joe didn't agree to it, and he stopped attending the council meetings for quite awhile. We've been watching Joe like a hawk lately. He's holed up in his place, but there's been a lot of coming and going the last few days."

"Anybody else?"

"It's hard to say. Whoever it is they've been patient,

and diligent. Rathcoate was under our radar, he was working for Harry on the side so we didn't know his value, but somebody did and they acted quickly. That speaks more to one or two individuals, not a larger group. There was no time to consult. Whoever killed him acted on their own impulse, and they acted fast."

"What are you people going to do about it?"

"Us? Nothing. You're the cop, it's up to you and your resources. We can't risk exposing the Consortium but it certainly has our attention. We're hoping you are good at your job Agent Tom Quinn."

"Right now, so am I."

No one spoke for a long interlude. The fire popped and snapped, the embers danced in pulsing waves. The evening had cooled and a wet dew had fallen while we talked. In spite of myself, I shivered, although I couldn't be sure if it was because of my situation or I was just chilly.

"What do you want me to do with the money?"

"Money?"

"Yes, Rathcoate had a second box. It had quite a bit of money in it."

"How much is 'quite a bit'?"

"Half a million, give or take. In unmarked bills. There is also some gold bullion and I kept the two flash drives and the letters that Harry wrote from the first box."

"Money can be a good thing to have. It opens doors and can make you some new friends."

"It's the new friends that I'm concerned about. If these people know so much, they probably know that there's money that is so far unaccounted for. They're going to be looking for it."

"All the more reason for you to have it and not me."
Charlie smiled across at him.

"Well then, I need a favor."

"Name it."

"I had to surrender my sidearm when I was put on leave. Does anyone have a gun I can borrow?"

Sally pushed herself up onto her feet and stretched her back.

"Let's get you back to Naperville. I'm pretty sure Jerry can fix you up. He likes those things. Charlie thank you for the hospitality and the information. When is the next meeting of the council?"

"It's not scheduled to meet right now. The events of the last few days though are going to raise some pretty serious paranoia. I suspect that a meeting will be called pretty soon now. They're going to want to know what precautions are being taken. We'll scramble and change passwords of course. They will start getting their enforcers amped up. We need to get a lid on this, and we need to get it done soon."

The Least of Your Worries

When we arrived back at the hotel, we were just in time to see my car leaving the parking garage on the back of a tow truck.

"What fresh hell is this?"

"Didn't you say you changed the license plates?" Greg spoke from the back seat.

"Yes, so what?"

"These parking garages out in the suburbs are dumps for stolen cars. Cars that people are looking for, especially the police. The hotels cooperate with the police departments and the police departments come through and do regular computer checks on the cars in the garage.

They're not usually this diligent, your car has only been there since just after noon today."

"So what are you saying. Somebody's already looking for me?"

"No, I didn't say that. They did a check on the plate and it didn't match the car, so they impounded it. But once they check the serial number then they're going to be looking for you. For sure. I think we better move you Tom. Did you register under your real name?"

"Yes."

"Jerry give him a gun. Then it looks like for you now, you're going to be bunking with me Tom."

"I can handle myself Sally. Just let me get grip on this, we're probably overreacting."

"Like you did for Rathcoate?"

"Good point. How about that gun Jerry?"

Jerry got out of the car and walked around to the back. Opening the hatch, he lifted the storage compartment lid in the floor. Inside was a small arsenal, there was a 12-guage riot gun with a pistol grip. There were two Glock nine millimeters, one with a silencer, an M-16/M4 with a night scope and a sawed-off double-barreled shotgun.

I took the Glock without the silencer and Jerry handed me a spare magazine which I pocketed. I racked the slide and a round popped out. Jerry caught it in the air and handed it back to me. I slid the holster into the waistband of my pants and adjusted.

"Are all these loaded and chambered?"

"Wouldn't be much good if they weren't."

Sally spoke up from the back seat. "Go get your stuff Tom. Take the stairs, don't go through the lobby, and meet us out in back when you come down."

I took the steps two at a time and then hurried down the hallway on the third floor and keyed the door to my room. When I opened the door, I was greeted with all the lights in the room shining brightly. Sitting in the chair at my desk was my SAC Dan Wilson, smoking a cigarette and smiling.

"Hello Tom. It would seem that you are in a lot more trouble than I already thought you were. Goodness but you've been busy."

"It's not what you think."

"Oh? Oh, I think it's exactly what I think it is."

Someone stepped into the room behind me and put a hand on my shoulder. With the other, they pulled the Glock with its holster out of my waistband. Then stepped around me and dropped the gun on the bed. Bob English sat down on the edge of the far bed and smiled, "Evening Tom."

"The reason that it's exactly what I think it is Tom, is because I'm writing the narrative. I'm about to solve a particularly nasty crime, and I'm about to experience a most excellent payday all on the same day."

"I recovered all of the money; I was going to turn it in as evidence. I just wanted to see if it led me anywhere else."

"Sure you did Tom. I'd expect nothing less from the son of Mickey Francis."

"You found out about my father?"

"I knew about your father, but I wanted to give you a chance to prove yourself Tom. Your bonafides were good; you scored well on your testing. I thought you eventually might be a good fit. Alas, we'll never find out now."

"I don't understand. If you knew about my father,

why'd you let me stay?"

"Because I needed you Tom. You were perfect for dealing with Harry. He would have been much more willing to talk with Mickey Francis' boy than some other new proby. No, it was a match made in heaven." He made a hard face and leaned forward, "Harry delivered. Now it's your turn. Where's the money Tom?"

"It's just evidence. It doesn't lead anywhere. There aren't any leads, I think Rathcoate was planning on getting away with it, but it doesn't seem to lead anywhere else."

"So I've guessed. But you're wrong Tom, because it led us right to you. I can't thank you enough really. A heinous murder committed and solved on the same day. And a sweet retirement bonus for yours truly. All wrapped up in a neat little package with a bow on top."

"What?"

"Come on Tom, you're a smart guy. Wake up and smell the coffee."

I looked at Dan Wilson. He was relaxed and smiling. Bob English was sitting with his arms crossed leaning back, comfortable. This didn't look like an arrest.

"You had Rathcoate murdered."

"Bingo. You're catching up."

"But how? I was with you the whole time."

"C'mon Tom, I was making phone calls for almost an hour organizing the task force. I had plenty of time to make a few calls of my own. I told you it was an interesting day didn't I? That was the beauty of it: I had the schedule. I knew when we would arrive at the Sheraton, I made sure there was plenty of time to get what we needed from him."

"No one deserves to die the way he did."

"Well we didn't know that you had moved the money and the files. We thought he was holding out on us. It's kind of funny really, apparently he tried like crazy to cooperate but couldn't because you'd already stolen his stuff. He couldn't have known that."

"Geezus."

"Now the only thing that's left is we have to deal with you Tom."

"Why?" I started imagining the last scene with J. J. Rathcoate; my palms started to sweat. Then I had a thought. "Have you ever been shot Dan?"

"Yes, once. Why?"

"Was it Harry?"

"Yes it was. Good for you Tom, you've started to connect the dots. Right when I had the son of a bitch right where I wanted him, he found a way to take the joy out of the situation

Yeah, I got a kick out of you talking about the sixth bullet all the time but you figured it out at last, didn't you. I knew right where that goddamn bullet was; in the top drawer of my desk. I could have showed it to you anytime I wanted. But I was having too much fun to spoil it before it was time.

"So here's the why. If we arrest you, you will have quite a bit to say. Not everything you have to say will matter, but some of it will. I'm only a few months from retirement; Bob here is actually overdue. We have both been waiting for a score like this to wind things up for us. Up until now everything has been penny ante, but this has got to be a goodly amount, and there's more where it came from.

"No, I'm sorry Tom, but you are extremely expendable. Your FBI career is already officially over. I filed the paperwork on it this afternoon while waiting for the APB on your car to return. But eliminating you fixes our narrative; solves all the riddles just the way we like them to be solved—permanently. Sadly, you resisted arrest and we will be required to use deadly force. Perfectly understandable considering the lethal capabilities of a trained FBI agent."

The door was right behind me. Bob English was leaning back on the bed and Dan Wilson had rocked back in the office chair. I grabbed the handle and jumped out into the hallway. Running down the hall I hoped they wouldn't chance shooting inside the hotel. I hit the door on the stairwell still alive and vaulted and jumped my way down the three flights of stairs and out into the night, but I had come out at the wrong end of the hotel. Sally, Greg and Jerry were waiting at the other end apparently because they were not here. Frantically I looked around and then hurried across the patio and deck and down onto the Riverwalk along the river. It was lower than the surrounding area and I hoped it would keep me out of site for a few minutes. I started walking, trying not to look like I was hurrying. I needed to get back around to the other end of the hotel.

After half a block I ducked into the shadows below one of the wooden pedestrian bridges spanning the river and looked back. It was late; most of the foot traffic of young parents with kids had gone home. The soft lighting of strategically placed period lighting fit the soft nighttime weather perfectly. There were a few couples strolling romantically and single people occupying benches staring at the river current bubbling over the rocks in the stream

Bob English stood out among the others, walking purposefully, scanning both sides of the water with his hand tucked inside his sweater.

I scrambled up a set of stone steps near the bridge, intending to cross the river and double back, but it was a dead end. The wooden structure ended in a circular area halfway across the river. It would be an excellent location for a theme wedding ceremony or Instagram selfies out over the river. I turned back just as a silhouette stepped into the entrance. Bob English dropped into a half crouch and held his gun in a two-handed grip as he slowly walked toward me.

"End of the line Tom."

Behind him another silhouette stepped into the entrance. This one was almost twice the size of Bob and moving quickly. In one motion, it closed the distance and encircled him in an embrace. Even at twelve or fifteen feet I heard the crack of Bob's neck and then the clatter of his gun as it fell on the wooden decking. I rushed forward and retrieved the gun.

Standing with one arm supporting Bob's inert form, Greg put a finger to his lips, signaling quiet.

"How many more?"

"Just one."

"Okay, I got this. Go get 'em."

"10-4 to that."

I crossed my arms as I walked back toward the hotel, attempting to shield the gun from view. No one was paying any attention as couples exchanged kisses in the half-light. I crossed the back of the hotel and rounded the corner to look for the SUV and Sally. It was sitting directly outside the stairwell door with the engine running quietly, but it was empty. I looked around, not sure of my next move.

"Turn around slowly Tom. Nothing quick, just nice and slow. Hands on the back of your head."

I stuck the gun in my waistband and put my hands up, but not all the way up and slowly turned. Dan Wilson stood in the decorative shrubbery along the edge of the building. He stepped out holding his gun steady.

"Nice try. But I figured you'd have another ride; all I had to do was wait for you to come back. Did you give Bob the slip?"

"Sort of."

"Take the gun out of your belt. Two fingers only. Drop it in the grass, then take two steps back."

"Aren't you worried I might be out of range?"

"Smart ass, not everyone is an ace on the range like you are. Don't worry, if I have to empty the magazine to hit you, it won't bother my conscience."

A shadow flitted forward from behind Wilson, the movements so fast that they blurred in the half-light. Dan Wilson coughed and took a step forward, then stumbled and went to his knees. He coughed again, jerking spasmodically like he was suddenly having a seizure. Finally, he fell face down in the wet grass, the jeweled handle of a knife protruding from the base of his skull. Behind him, Sally Carlisle still stood in a half crouch.

"Go get the boys Tom. It's time to go."

Reflections

The hearing had been a formality. It was pretty clear that my father had been a career criminal and that it would have been less than believable that I could not have known. It was not enough in and of itself, but after the fiasco with J.J. Rathcoate, it was another and final nail in my coffin. The last straw was the discovery of two venerable FBI agents found dead together in a hotel room with almost a quarter of a million dollars in the western suburbs that I was tied to. There was no DNA evidence to put me at the scene, but the room across the hallway was registered in my name, so there were suspicions. I cleaned out my desk and went home to contemplate my future.

There would be more questions, some that I didn't have good answers for, but there dewas nothing that I could be arrested for. It was clear that any career in law enforcement was over for me, and I had never contemplated any other one. I decided it was time to have that talk with my father.

I had trouble finding them. I had not been there in a couple years and my memory was tenuous. Somewhere in the back of my mind, I probably didn't want to remember the directions. In an odd admittance to myself, I didn't want to admit that I was alone in this world. But I finally admitted defeat and consulted the directory to locate them.

The rain had been unrelenting, days of intense airless heat and high sky interspersed with periods of intense rain, thunder and gale force wind, typical July weather for the Chicago area. After three months of dreary snow squalls and high winds, the promise of spring was already past. Now it would be summer's heat until late August. All over the city, senior citizens would suffer the fatal combination of heat and low income housing. The obituaries would show a seasonal uptick and the obituary pages of the Chicago Tribune would be filled with 'died peacefully at home' entries.

I had trouble finding them. I had not been there in a couple years and my memory was tenuous. Somewhere in the back of my mind, I probably didn't want to remember the directions. In an odd admittance to myself, I didn't want to admit that I was alone in this world. But I finally admitted defeat and consulted the directory to locate them.

I had never really understood the purpose of cemeteries, a memorial garden where you planted a loved one's remains and then over the next generation, slowly forgot that they had ever existed. It had always seemed like a waste of good acreage to me.

Now I stood in the rain, looked down at their modest headstone, and tried to feel a connection to the stone, if not the bones beneath my feet. Kathleen Elizabeth Quinn, Mother, Grandmother, Friend

That she had been. The neighborhood mother we all ran to when we'd been injured. The woman who could pull you onto her lap and rock you to comfort. The woman who ruled with a drawn eyebrow demanded absolute silence during Sunday mass. A person who demanded clean underwear whenever we left home and shrugged away most transgressions with society's rules. A woman who had called the shots across the entire rest of the neighborhood.

Michael Francis Quinn, Father. I looked at the stone, reaching for the memory and the cornerstone of our relationship. He was there, always there in my memory. Bigger in my concept, as I suppose all fathers are, but a shadow dodging in and out of memory. Memories of his silhouette in the living room in the dark of the night, sitting in his chair, smoking cigarettes and drinking whiskey straight from the bottle that sat on the floor next to him. My father, his booming laugh echoing in my ears when times were good. A dark hero reflecting no warmth to anyone.

I sat on a facing headstone and looked down at the two of them. Mom had gone first. The diligence to her portion of the stone made that clear. She would have made those arrangements even as the cancer slowly ate her from the inside out. She would have placed the order and written the check. The inscriptions on stone encapsulated volumes of dialog. It was my mother's stone; my father had eventually just shown up. I knew I should feel something, I figured I must or I would not have wanted to come here in the first place. When I thought about my mother, I understood her challenging life. Raising kids in a strange city oh so far away from the little dirt farm where she had grown up. Somehow, and only with the strength of her own character, she managed to raise her children and triumph in the neighborhood. Then only to watch all but one of them die. She had been the doting grandmother to every kid in the neighborhood but didn't live long enough to see any of her own in spite of her greatest hopes. Eventually, inevitably dying from the heartbreak of that realization.

I considered my father. He had been solid, or so I had thought, and he had died a free man. He had apparently been pretty good at his chosen profession and had successfully kept it a secret from his children. He had been quick with a joke and casually athletic. That much I remembered. His photographs, what few there were, showed a handsome man, slightly shorter than his wife with a broad smile.

I reached into my pocket and took out a fresh pack of cigarettes and a small butane lighter. I had not smoked a cigarette since I had left the army, but I had missed them every day. Today I was going to smoke a cigarette with my dad and maybe have a conversation about how he had managed to fuck me up.

I understood that it might take more than one cigarette.

Epilogue

The warm rain had long since soaked through all my clothing and filled my shoes. The gravestone I was sitting on conversely felt cold through my soaked pants and underwear. I had smoked a couple of cigarettes too quickly and now I sat staring at nothing, feeling the nauseating distress of nicotine and an empty stomach.

I had spent the time reflecting on my parents' and my life. Remembering all the times that should have raised questions as I was growing up, and all the times that were lost. I'd wished my siblings back and sadly wondered if it would have made any difference in my life choices.

Now it was time to go. Back to my little studio apartment above the pizza joint and my endless litany of woulda', shoulda' and coulda' that would be my life for the foreseeable future.

Movement in my peripheral vision drew my attention and I looked up. Walking between the stones was an older gentleman carrying a large open black umbrella. As he slowly approached, he looked from one stone to another but didn't linger over any one of them. As I sat watching him, he never looked up, but I could tell he was coming my way.

In no particular hurry apparently, it was a full five minutes before he arrived. Standing behind my parents' headstone he reached into his pocket and took out a few coins. Selecting one, he placed it on my father's side of the stone and stood there silently looking down at it for a few moments.

I said nothing, content in my sodden misery to wonder at this unforeseen development. He was well dressed in a dark suit and tie. His black umbrella matched the black trenchcoat he wore. His face was not young, but was pink and healthy with very few smile lines. When he looked up his eyes were bright and there was no laughter behind them.

"Hello Thomas."

"Do I know you?"

"No, I don't think so, but you will I hope."

"I don't need any new friends right now."

"I'm pretty sure that a new friend is exactly what you need right now."

"And what makes you think that."

"Because, you don't have very many right now. At least that right kind of friend anyway."

"And what kind of friend would that be?"

"The kind that could help."

"And just exactly who are you, if I might ask." My stomach was not getting any better.

"I am the best kind of friend to have. A friend in the right place."

"Thanks but I'm not shopping these days."

"I was a good friend of your father's. He might disagree."

"Great! Just another chapter that I haven't read yet."

He reached into the inside pocket of his suit coat and drew out a piece of paper. Stepping around the stone, he held it at arm's length handing it to me. It was a letter, hand-written and I recognized the script. It was Harry's handwriting.

"Harry asked me to look you up."

"Who the hell are you?"

"My name is Frank Lattoria. Harry told me you know how to keep a secret."

www.ingramcontent.com/pod-product-compliance
Lightning Source LLC
Chambersburg PA
CBHW060241100726
47907CB00003B/723